Two-Headed

Dragon

AUTHOR'S NOTE

This novel contains content that may be sensitive. Due to the rules and restrictions of publishing with the 'zon, please always read the description of content on the author's website.

First edition published 2023
ISBN: 9798870725727

Cover illustrations copyright © 2023 by Rosel Graphic Designs
Edited by Lawrence Editing

Published by Delilah Dare
www.delilahdarebooks.com

To the *good girls* who like to be a little naughty.

When treasure falls into a dragon's lair, it rightfully belongs to the dragon who dwells there.

Chapter 1

Dana

You won't be fertile forever, you know. I really want us to start thinking seriously about our future family."

Jackson's words drifted past Dana through the mountain air, which was becoming more and more crisp as they made their ascent. This hiking trip through the Rockies was supposed to bring them closer together, but he kept spewing the same rhetoric about her *fertile eggs* as always and pushing her to get a job to support a nonexistent family.

"You should tell the temp agency tomorrow that you

need something long-term and sustainable for kids, especially something with upward mobility. Ask about the maternity program."

"Okay."

"Are you even listening to me?" Jackson whirled on her. A rock scuttled from underneath his thickly treaded boot. Dana watched as it jumped over any pebbles in its way and passed between her feet to make a turbulent escape down the mountain pass.

"Of course I am, Jackson," she exasperated. She slipped her glasses off and wiped the lenses on her athletic tank top, causing even more streaks to line her eyesight when the plastic frames settled back onto her nose. She ignored them and walked past him with a practiced calm.

At this point in the three years they'd been together, she'd become an expert at tuning him out. Much like the way he tuned *her* out every time she reiterated that she didn't want kids. The cosmos only knew who was winning the argument, although it appeared Jackson had already decided.

She was as afraid of dying alone as the next person, but that wasn't the reason she stuck around. Jackson had supported her as she followed her passion for writing. At least financially, he'd supported her dreams of authorhood while she made very little income to contribute. If not for him, she would be living with her mom and sister in her hometown of Witmore, likely driving to and from Colorado Springs with a part-time job and writing only when she had the time.

She owed Jackson a great deal for how much he'd done for her. If not for her sense of guilt and duty, maybe she would have left. As it was, she was beginning to wear down.

They paused at the lowest peak on this trail, which was still a decent summit. Jackson slipped his arms around her waist from behind. The gesture was so gentle, she leaned into it and thought, *maybe I'm being ridiculous.* At twenty-seven years old, she knew plenty of women her age who were happy to be mothers. Her friend Cicily had an unexpected pregnancy and she constantly preached about it being the best thing to ever happen in her life.

Maybe it could be that way for Dana, too.

Jackson sighed. "This view is great. The only thing that would make it better would be if my hands were resting all the way out *here*"—he held his hands out as though her belly were bigger than a basketball—"instead of this flat strip."

"Right, like I would be climbing mountains if I were a whale," she snorted. Leave it to Jackson to remind her exactly why she didn't want to waver on the kids thing just as she was considering giving in.

Thankfully, Jackson was utterly predictable and couldn't go a full five minutes without reminding her she was a baby farm. With a shake of her head, she reached for her glasses as he retreated from her backside. It must be the altitude messing with her head, tricking her into believing his little gestures could be anything other than ploys to get his way.

The ground scraped under his feet somewhere behind her. His hands firmly met her shoulder blades and he grunted with effort as he shoved her off the mountain.

There was no time for anger or shock. Wind surged past with too much force for her limbs to fight, the noisy rush deafening. She hardly registered that she was falling, but her body took the beating of the cliffside. Not far down, she hit a slab of flat cliff with enough force to steal the breath from her lungs. The impact slowed her descent significantly and she slid, then tumbled on her side until she reached brush. She rolled and rolled, her whole body scraping and chafing as she bowled through the brush.

Her body was limp and battered by the time she reached level ground, rolled down a small incline, and plummeted deep into a bear cave.

"Asshole!" she shouted when she realized she was alive. Every bone and muscle in her body screamed with pain, her synapses on fire. The fact that she was alive was a miracle.

"That cock-sucking *bajingan*! *Jancok kon*!"

She lay still and checked in with her body. Her elbow felt funky and didn't want to move from its crooked position. That's fine, she could live without an arm, right? Blood covered her in many places, a whole chunk of skin missing from her thigh. It was grotesque to look at but didn't feel broken. It would definitely get uglier before healing.

If not for the cliff a couple yards down breaking her fall along with her tuck-and-roll skills, she would have died. Had that been Jackson's plan for this trip all along? Or had it been a spur of the moment thing? Agree to have his babies or die, apparently. She'd narrowly dodged that bullet. Moments before he pushed her, she'd truly considered giving in. That fucker almost got his way.

Her aching muscles revolted as she lugged herself into a seated position. With a full-body wince, she reached for her glasses but came up with empty air. *Great! Just what I need.* She would have to come up with money for new glasses on top of everything.

Okay, okay. She could do this. She just needed to climb out of the sloped tunnel and blindly find her way out of the woods. This was the same park they always hiked. She could get to the trail and find her way to the convenience store to call a car. Luckily, her pack and supplies seemed to have survived with her. If she made it home tonight, she could at least grab some personal items and her only remaining pair of contacts before heading to her mom's house in the morning. The bastard was probably going to continue his hike and stay at the lodge for the next couple nights as planned, because why not?

A large, strangely shaped red rock took up most of the discernible area of the cave, but there were piles of junk strewn about as well. Shiny objects glinted and vied for her unfocused eye. Peculiar items, sparkly things that wouldn't usually be found in an underground cave, even if someone were squatting there.

"Weird."

The textured rock moved. Two long, thick pillars of

crimson extracted themselves from the main lump and moved forward, sending her scrambling back with a hiss of pain.

Two sets of eyes settled on her. Dana frantically looked between them, her neck whiplashing from side to side as all four eyes blinked slowly. A translucent membrane slid across the slitted irises followed by a heavy red lid. Both snouts dragged in deep breaths that commanded the air around her, sucking her tattered sleeves up toward them. Long, thin, forked pink tongues flicked out from both mouths, revealing double-lined rows of teeth as they dragged over dry lips.

Dana screamed. She catapulted out of there as fast as she could. She ignored the blazing hot pain in her elbow as she leaned on it to climb and the searing open wound of her leg as she stumbled.

She ran and ran and didn't look back, too terrified to consider that there were other things in these woods willing to eat her.

Chapter 2

Rathym

Fire was always a mesmerizing subject to Rathym. As a Fireborn, he'd grown up steeped in the traditions of the Great Flame. Fire poured from his throat with a familiar burn as he used the flames to rebuild and reshape the mountain. Fireborn were notoriously strong-willed and stubborn, forces to be reckoned with just like their element.

With the assistance of an ancient potion, Fireborn had been using their fire to hide in plain sight for millennia. Although the mountain rock was not hot to his touch, it glowed under his flames like embers of lava. Their bright orange mimicked the package aglow in the corner of his eye, mocking him with every glance he sent its way.

This latest mountain was more malleable than the ones before. The solid rock above him thundered and groaned under his ministrations, the enormous formation working double-time to resist his changes.

Rathym would not be moving his lair again. This was the last time. He hadn't been alive for over five centuries just to lie down and surrender his hard-earned things. This new home would be his, his alone, for his remaining time alive. If the human population continued to encroach, he would raze their cities to the ground. He would not consider returning to his traitorous homeland, not even if his stomach turned to ice and no fire graced his mouth again.

Besides, his collection of valuables had grown so massive that it was a pain to keep lugging around to new mountains.

Not that he didn't love sorting through his belongings. He did. He enjoyed the act of setting them up along the walls, creating shelving units in the stone to adorn with beautiful things, sorting the rest into piles. He loved to reminisce over his cherished treasures.

He *didn't* love to reminisce about his past. The shimmering orange summons hummed from its discarded spot on the dining table. The ghosts that haunted him had spent centuries looming in the back of his mind, but now they threatened to implode their thresholds.

With an aggravated harrumph, Rathym nudged the magic-laced parcel onto the floor and swiftly kicked it under the table. He would deal with it later. Right now, his new home required his full attention. A convenient distraction.

A distraction he'd been reliant on for nearly a week. He would have to open the parcel soon and assess the importance of its contents. The Fire Council would not contact him now, two centuries after his hostile departure, if the circumstances weren't dire. It was possible that he'd already procrastinated too long, rendering any aid he could provide useless.

Fortunately, there was no one alive in that realm that he still felt a responsibility to save.

The new cave was large enough to accommodate an additional pile. An exciting venture. What should he categorize into the new space? Perhaps by rank of beauty? A pile for enchanted items already existed, as did elven treasures gifted to Rathym before the fall of the great species. Other piles included gold, silver, and things that were just rather neat. He was sure to come up with something.

He backed into a corner to examine his handiwork. It was adequate, but would be more aesthetically pleasing once he finished decorating.

His tail bumped something under the table. In his recklessness, he'd positioned the summons in a horrible place. He quickly moved his tail, but the damage was done. The parcel now bore a gash in its packaging. It would be a matter of time before the whole parcel vanished, whether he'd read it or not.

"Cursed flame!" Rathym swore as he downshifted and snatched the folder. There was no way to know how quickly it would disappear. That depended on how classified the information was. Of course, if he were still in possession of his council-appointed signet ring, he would be able to force the enchanted parcel to remain even after its expiration.

Unfortunately, his ring was long gone. Anything inside the thick folder would dissipate after whatever length of time the council had deemed appropriate.

A stack of papers almost an inch thick goaded him. What could they possibly want from Rathym that required this much parchment? He eased the first piece from the front and began to read.

Sir Rathym Odrydimere, Grand Commander of the Fire Sworn Elite Forces, Regent to the Young Princess of Elvendale…

"*Former*," he grumbled.

A muffled scream alerted him to a presence near his home's entrance. He immediately shifted back into his larger form, prepared to stand his ground when the intruder descended.

These cozy living quarters came equipped with a hidden entrance—a hole disguised as a burrow. He'd decided it had to be his immediately. All the better to keep prying human pests away. Although it had been a challenge to load his hoard through. He'd had to make a sort of back entrance that he promptly destroyed with an intentional rockfall the following day, which rearranged much of the mountain into staggered cliffs.

The petrified scream hurtled down the tunnel entrance and landed with a painful sounding thud.

A new precious item for my collection.

Rathym was an old-fashioned dragon and understood perfectly what it meant when something fell into his lair.

Very slowly, he placed the stack of parchment on the table. Careful not to scare the puny thing, he stood perfectly still and observed their reaction to this unsettling new arrangement.

This new piece of treasure was enchanting indeed. Their features rivaled those of any elf from Elvendale. Other than their phenomenal bone structure, however, they seemed ill-equipped for survival. They fumbled around like a blind mouse searching for scraps at a picnic, not to mention their delicious scent was sure to draw the ravenous beasts from their depths in the woods.

After he was content that he'd spent enough time observing his new jewel and had provided it with adequate time to adjust, he leaned in for closer inspection.

A human of female persuasion. He dragged in a deep breath of her scent to confirm. Yes, it was a distinctly powerful female pheromone. Even as a sweaty musk, it smelled so tantalizing he couldn't help but lick his lips.

She shrieked and clamored away, crawling awkwardly and inefficiently out of his entryway.

The little human ran from his lair, undoubtedly believing they'd made their escape.

Every muscle in his body told him to chase after her, but out of the corner of his eyes, he noticed the Council's folder emit a faint gold light. Annoyed, he downshifted and forced his attention back to the letter.

It pleases us to inform you that there has been a breakthrough in the investigation of King Luvon Ludove's assassination.

A break? Could that possibly mean...
Rathym read the words again before continuing.

It pleases us to inform you that there has been a breakthrough in the investigation of King Luvon Ludove's assassination. The murderer, Ivaan Kovgroff, is being held in the Iron Forge Prison and will face his reckoning in a fortnight.

Enclosed in this folder is the complete classified account of the investigation and all applicable paperwork, including the Fire Court's transcription from the trial, as per your original request—

Gold spots ate away at the parchment in his hands. The bottom half of the stack engulfed in cold flames. Rathym barely caught the date marked in the topmost corner before the light vanished and his claws were empty.

The vile creature that murdered his closest friend over two centuries ago would finally be held accountable. The one who'd forced little Riniya to be an orphan princess with an unqualified dragon regent would *finally* face his reckoning.

It was good news.

Yet, Rathym's hearts ached. Not only was Luvon long dead, but the entire realm of elves was gone, lost to the void by the hands of an incompetent human invader who fancied himself a magician. Although the only evidence from the scene made it clear dear Luvon was killed by a Fireborn dragon, the Fire Council discarded the investigation after the elves were lost. Rathym had made a very public, rather unprofessional demand that they solve the murder of their greatest ally else they lose their Grand Commander. Which they ignored. Hence his mundane life in the land of humans, hopping from cave to cave like an imbecile.

As he paced, something glinted inside the entrance. He downshifted into his smaller reptilian form and plucked the item from the tunnel. Spectacles. One sniff and he knew they would be sufficient for tracking his human intruder.

The human would have to wait, but he was not letting them go. There were matters he must attend first, but he would never allow one of his possessions to run away like that.

Especially not the most enrapturing item he owned.

Chapter 3

Dana

For the second time that day, Dana experienced the miraculous hand of the universe. She found her way to the tourist trap of a town and ordered a ride to the home she shared with Jackson in Colorado Springs. Knowing him as well as she did, she had no doubt Jackson would keep gallivanting through the mountains, acting like nothing had happened. Well, screw him. She wouldn't even bother texting him that she'd lived through his little dateline scheme. She'd just stay home tonight, pack her things, and after her interview in the morning, she would grab what she could and stay with her mom and sister.

As for what happened in the bear cave—nope, nope,

nope. She hadn't had her glasses on. It could've been some kind of lizard. That stood on an invisible rock to meet her eye level. With two heads the size of her torso. What was she supposed to do? Call animal control?

After a long, tear-filled shower—both from anger and the pain of her wounds being hit with pressurized water—she gathered some of her crap and put it in the corner for easy retrieval. Jackson wasn't an idiot. Not completely. Surely he'd realize her stuff was missing and understand she was alive. She should probably consider pressing charges. What an absolute jerk for making her deal with this.

Her dreams were angsty. Full of betrayal and babies that looked like little mini-jerks. *Gah! I hate babies!* That was a bit of a hyperbole. What she meant was, she hated babies who didn't belong to her friends—key word, *friends*.

In the morning, her head was groggy and slow. She dreaded the upcoming day. She could skip the temp agency appointment, but that would mean a more permanent living situation with her family. While she strongly believed that needing support and allowing that support to come from family members was perfectly okay, she preferred her independence. Not to mention a grown-up bedroom as opposed to the teenage poster-plastered walls of her youth. Not to mention space from her mom's high expectations and subtle criticism.

Her contacts didn't help. They'd been worn once or twice and her astigmatism made it difficult to adjust even though they'd been kept in the heavy-duty solution from her optometrist. Everything was a bit fuzzy at the edges of her vision, which only accentuated the fuzz inside her head. She stuffed the contact case and solution in her bag, along with eye drops.

Hopefully she wouldn't make a total bimbo of herself at the temp office. Without Jackson's financial support, her writing career was basically tanked. Not that her readers would be too surprised considering the length of her writing slump. Jackson had spent most of his time "supporting" her by simultaneously reproaching her, which didn't help her imposter syndrome at all.

"Those books give you women unrealistic ideas of relationships," he'd say. Then he would add, "Men like that don't exist."

She'd long since given up trying to explain that women don't actually *want* all of the tropes in romance books. They're often an exaggeration of reality that wouldn't be acceptable in real life. In reality, the arrogant boss-hole would get a sexual assault charge. Well, hopefully, at least.

But it wasn't only romance books that he had a problem with. He had issues with fantasy novels, too, saying things like, "Those books fill your head with nonsense."

Needless to say, it really dampened her creativity.

Get your head straight! She urged the woman in the mirror while furiously combing her freshly box-dyed brown hair cropped above her shoulders, awkwardly flaring at the bottoms and in need of a cut. She didn't often wear makeup, but her blotchy complexion and the dark bags under her brown eyes required she do so today. It was a warm day out, but she would have to wear pants to cover the huge chunk of missing skin on her leg. She would have to wrap it, too, so it didn't bleed through.

Her bicycle coasted down the hill. The pleasant sensation *would* have helped rid her mind of the resentful thoughts and the dread filling her chest cavity, if not for the searing pain of her injuries. When she reached the building, she stiffened to minimize the pain as she kicked out the bike stand and locked it up.

"Good morning! Name, please?" the woman at the front desk chirped.

"Hello. I'm Dana Gretchens."

"Take a seat and fill this out. Bring it back up when you're done."

"Thanks," she said cheerily and accepted the form.

A few minutes later, an impeccably dressed woman in high heels called out her name and led her to a cubicle covered in little pig figurines. She peered at Dana through black-and-white checkered glasses. Suddenly, Dana felt her whole personality was underdressed.

"So, Dana...Gretchens," the woman said with a glance at the clipboard. "I've reviewed your information and I believe we have a perfect fit for you!"

"Oh, really? That's great news!" Ignoring the sharp pain in her arm, Dana leaned forward, eager to find out what the perfect fit was. Did they have a creative writing job? Even something a little more technical would be fine, as long as she got to write. She loved stringing words together.

"It is! Wonderful. Can you start tomorrow?"

"Well, yes. What's the job?"

"It's a customer service representative position at Fielding Collections Corp. Early morning hours are available, full time, full benefits, and they have a wonderful maternity program!"

Oh. My. God.

This had to be the reason the universe had provided so many miracles lately. For this joke, right here, this punch line delivered directly to her face by an eccentric temp agency worker. The universe was literally laughing in her face.

Dana simply smiled. She choked down her disappointment and the wild urge to burst out laughing. She leaned back and nodded emphatically, as though the lady was absolutely right, a collections representative was her destiny. Her true calling. The perfect fit.

"Okay. I'll take it!"

"Oh, wonderful! I'll email you the details. Be there on time or early and make us proud!"

"Wonderful." Dana watched the woman light up even brighter with her seemingly favorite word stated back to her.

Well, that could've gone worse. They could have turned her away entirely. Although the irony was palpable.

She needed to use the restroom, but she had to get out of this godforsaken building first. The more she ignored the pain of her elbow, her aching muscles, and the open sore of her leg, the worse it hurt. She couldn't guarantee she'd be able to stifle her groans while easing down onto a toilet seat.

Unable to throw her leg over the bike, she gripped the handles with white knuckles and grimaced all the way down the few streets leading to a park. As she leaned into the turn, she noticed a large bird circling overhead. Squinting to make out something that far in her contacts, all she could see was a big, fuzzy red lump.

Crimson. Oh, God! She'd almost forgotten about that cave. The memory sent a shiver down her spine. She didn't really want to think about that. It had to have been a hallucination, right?

She leaned her bike against the community bathroom building and double-checked that the stick person on the sign wore a triangle dress. It wouldn't be the first time she couldn't see well enough and walked into the men's.

She entered the last stall and eased onto the toilet, keeping her scraped leg stiff and straight. Someone came in as she finished, so she held in her tears, pulled up her pants, and slung her backpack over her shoulder.

A monstrous growl snatched her attention. The toilet in the stall beside her flushed. The door opened with a squeak. The woman's scream pierced the air, followed by an inhuman roar.

Dana's stall door flew across the room and slammed against the opposite wall, narrowly missing her nose.

There stood a humanoid reptile the color of blood. It lumbered into her stall and loomed above her, so tall that the largest horns of its spiked crown scraped the ceiling with a force that had chips of debris falling to the ground. The reptilian form stooped down to her, close enough for her to make out his features perfectly.

Its body was covered in scales, with the torso of an abnormally ripped bodybuilder and an entirely inhuman amount of abdomen muscles. Its nose was more like a snout, but the feature she gravitated to the most were its gorgeous eyes. The left was yellow with a burst of red around the pupil, while the right had two irises fused together, the colors of coconut jam and cherries bleeding into each other like watercolor paints.

What was this creature? Some kind of reptile, or some ancient deity?

Dana was as starstruck as she'd been that time Beyoncé made eye contact with her. She was so entranced with its peculiar eyes when it dragged in a deep nose-full of her neck. Her eyelids fluttered closed, a shiver trickling down her spine. She stumbled forward and opened her eyes, which locked on something over the creature's shoulder. *Wings?*

She stepped back and subconsciously reached for her glasses to wipe them on her shirt. It took a few pinches of her forefinger and thumb to remember they weren't on her face.

Those captivating eyes stayed intent on her, dancing with something she couldn't pinpoint.

"I'm here to bring you home." The rumbling voice sounded simultaneously like thunder and a melody, like the banging of tribal drums in the pouring rain.

"Wha—oh!"

She was thrust over a scaly shoulder, a claw-tipped hand firmly positioned on her ass. The next moment, they burst through the roof of the brick building and took off into the air.

She watched as the wings elongated. Broad shoulders lengthened along with the entire expanse of his scale-covered back. A tail she hadn't noticed before now spanned thrice her height. She grasped at pointed spikes and turned to see two heads at the end of long, thick necks, and then it hit her.

She was riding on the back of a literal dragon.

Chapter 4
Rathym

The flight home was a frustrating one. The human's honey and ambrosial scent taunted Rathym with every flap of his wings, the female's pheromones heightened by her adrenaline. She had no right to smell as enticing as she did. Humans were nuisances. He'd never considered one might smell so delectable, yet here she was, throwing that sweet scent in his face.

The effect she had on him was beyond a mild annoyance. It was utterly undeniable while in his downshift, requiring him to immediately expand into full form the moment they reached the bottom of the tunnel. The absolute overwhelm of all his senses could only be a sign of one thing.

There were very few species still around that relied on mate bonds. Even back when he was young, the dependence of mate bonds was fading. Too many mates were rejected, cast away in favor of *true love*. Just because two bodies are compatible biologically doesn't mean their hearts will align.

When dragons encountered their mate, it wasn't unusual for one of their shifts to have a stronger reaction than the other. The flooding of the senses signified they were in the presence of their ideal partner. But a dragon had never mated with a human, as far as his knowledge. A dragon and a human could not conceive, so how could the mate bond perceive them as *biologically* compatible? He was not about to break centuries of tradition for a fluke.

Nor would he allow his belongings to stray from their designated places. He shoved aside the irksome matter of her scent and mulled over what pile he would assign this new, shiny, delicious object to. He maintained his full shift to dampen the mating urges as he glanced between the female and the towering heaps of treasure in deliberation.

"Oh! You saved them for me!" the human squealed.

Her lack of fear surprised Rathym. He'd sniffed the faintest trace of it upon initial retrieval, and again when they were in flight, but since returning her feet to the ground, it had faded.

He scanned the woman's face for a hint as to what she referred to. Her gaze was fixated on the claw still clutching the spectacles he'd used to track her scent. She gingerly pried them from his claw and surveyed the damaged lens, her mouth pursing tightly as she wiggled the frames. She produced a small rag from her knapsack and rubbed the unbroken lens with fervor. When she placed them on her nose, the right side protruded from her brow.

"I'm sure I can get them fixed." She shrugged and folded them on her collar. She beamed at him. "Thank you."

Taken aback by her gratitude, he allowed her to believe he'd done as she said. Intelligent critters like this needed assurances, as they were easier to keep safe when they were aware of their dragon's care for them.

Returning to the task at hand, Rathym considered each mound of stuff, occasionally glancing at the woman to compare her against them.

"What are you doing?"

"Appraising my new treasure."

"What's your new treasure?" she inquired with an innocent lilt that would be endearing if it didn't annoy him so much.

She would be the first talking treasure he owned— well, other than the enchanted smock, but that ego-bruising cloth was overpriced and underwhelming. A painful mockery of art. He would toss it out with the compost if it didn't rightfully belong to him. Whether worn for cooking duties or oil painting, nothing he created was ever good enough to please the damned thing. It made for poor company.

Although, that did give him an idea. Perhaps the

human would be happiest in the area allocated to enchanted items. If she became lonesome, she need only activate the smock. Humans thought highly of their clothing, using it to appease their prudish nature. In all of his centuries, he'd yet to encounter an uncovered human, all of them body shy and excessively modest.

With a deep breath to ease his annoyance, he gestured to her.

"You trespassed into my home. That makes you *mine*." He ground his teeth against the twinge of pain that came with having to repeat himself. He hadn't had to speak so much in centuries, and he was a great listener—alas, to himself, at least. "Have I not made that clear?"

Her eyes expanded wider than the silver elven platters that leaned against the armoire behind her, which stole Rathym's attention over her shoulder. That was not where the elven silver belonged. He would remedy the oversight.

The human made a strangled sound somewhere between choking and laughing. She pinched the air beside her temples. Was that a tic? A malfunction? She fidgeted a moment longer before lifting her spectacles from her blouse and scrubbing the good lens with the little slip of cloth. All the while, she blubbered strange, incoherent nonsense that had Rathym's eyes slamming into slits.

"Out with it, human."

"I'm sure we can figure this out. This is—this is all, all a misunderstanding." She laughed again. "I don't belong to anyone. I'm a person!"

"A person who undeniably crashed into my lair." How irritating. He narrowed one set of eyes at her, the other drifting back to his task. "I know the code. You are *mine*. All of my things belong here, in my home, with me. At all times."

She defiantly placed her hands on her hips and sputtered. "What about when you're away?"

"My things remain in their designated area."

"I can't stay here. I need a bed, and a fridge, and— and a bathroom!"

Both of his heads turned to her and he huffed. Her pointless arguments were tiresome and he was already exhausted.

"Nonsense. There are plenty of comfortable places in our home to lay your head. I will provide you with food, of course. The lavatory is two rooms down."

Her jaw dropped open. His attention immediately snapped to the slope of her mouth. That uncanny sensation welled within him again, as though his mate were near and beckoned his hearts to their side. He yanked himself away so quickly he almost slammed his necks against each other.

"I'm certain you'll find it more than habitable. Although, I have moved quite often in this past century. Some of my favorite pieces are hidden or…misplaced." He attempted to smile at her but flinched at the foreign stretch of his lips. "I'm sure you will fit right in. For now, I am weary. I'm not as spry as I used to be. Perhaps you'll have an easier time determining where you fit than if I were to decide for you."

On that note, Rathym retreated to his nest of silks, linens, pillows, blankets, and mattresses in the northeast corner of his home. The little sleeping cove provided a lovely view of all his belongings, their colors and textures a comforting quilt of beauty. His eyelids grew heavy as his midday nap began to relax the muscles in his body.

Movement kept his heavy lids from closing. He jolted awake. The human was rubbing his prized golden urn with the rag she'd used on her spectacles. While he was too horror-stricken to react, she moved on to an elven silver vase in the adjoining pile.

"What are you doing? Cease that at once! You cannot—do not use inferior cloth to shine elven silver!" He rose from his nest in a huff and jogged toward her, using his broad, rightmost head to nudge her aside and block her with his neck, restraining her against the cold wall. With his other pair of eyes, he assessed the damage done. Nothing noticeable. Thank the Great Flame he'd caught her in time. "I thought I told you to find a place to sit!"

"Elven?"

"Yes, elven! Did you think I held menial items in such high regard? Everything you see here is a treasure in its own right, and you shall treat them with respect!"

Her brows rocketed to the top of her head and her plump lips were framed by darkened cheeks. Rathym growled with irritation at the wave of heat it sent reeling through him. His body responded to the human's beauty even while he was incredibly upset with her. *Traitorous spark.*

"I'm sorry. I didn't know. But if they're so treasured, why are they all just lying around?"

Cursed flame, what have I done to deserve this? The woman was proving a pain in his side, and yet she had the audacity to look like *that* while she ridiculed his very way of life! Must he explain everything to her? How was he to start from the beginning of ancient tradition and make it to the end without giving in to the carnal need her presence coaxed from his spark?

For the first time, Rathym longed to disregard the code and send her away. Far, far away, where the forge within him would not ignite from her nearness and he would not have to suffer any more of these questions.

A grumbling sound like that of a wee bear cub attempting to mimic their fierce mother's growl emitted from the human's body. She clutched her stomach.

She was hungry already.

"I'll hunt. Stay put, human, so that I do not have to track you down again. Understood?"

She nodded and leaned against the silver vase. "Understood, um…what do I call you?"

"Rathym."

"I'm Dana."

"Dana. Remain here or I will be forced to hunt you down again."

Rathym downshifted and shot through the tunnel before she could come up with another question. He needed to put space between them. Maybe enough distance would dull the strange feelings simmering within him.

Distance. How would he achieve proper distance when she was to live in his dwelling?

Chapter 5
Dana

The formidable two-headed dragon's form shrank, then disappeared out the tunnel in a flurry of crimson wings and claws, leaving her alone in the dank cave that smelled like an earthen musk.

Dana leaned against a huge vase to ease the strain on her scabbing leg. The vase was incredibly sturdy and came all the way up to her elbow. Why would elves need silver vases this large? Did they make them specifically for the dragons?

She snorted at her inner dialogue. *Elves and dragons.* What else was out there? Would she get to find out?

On one hand, she could try to escape while he was away. Worst-case scenario, she wouldn't make it to town before he caught her scent again. *Best*-case scenario, he would destroy Jackson's house while retrieving her. She wasn't sure what tier of insurance Jackson paid for, but she doubted it would cover a dragon destroying the roof.

On the other hand, she couldn't help feeling a bit of a thrill that the *nonsense* in her fantasy novels was real, and she was living it. A dragon had not only shown her his lair but also seemed to take pride in her presence there. Sure, he was a grumpy old dragon with a prickly personality, but she would be out of her mind not to seize this opportunity. It was miles better than the alternative. Returning to her normal life, which had just imploded in her face. She'd spent so long stifling her personality, her passion, just to please those around her. She wasn't in a rush to return to the nightmare of reality.

At least for now, she would go with this strange new flow. Tomorrow, she had to get to the collections agency to start her first day.

Oh, crap! She'd forgotten about her new job. Still, she wouldn't make it very far on an empty stomach. It was best to make her escape after the grouchy beast fell asleep. Once he was snoring, she would sneak away and return to her humdrum life. Which would now include calling old folks and college students to demand their money like some kind of legal burglar.

While Dana was stuck in her musings about an uncertain and rather unappealing future, Rathym returned with a stag thrown over his shoulder and sauntered farther into the cave. Curious to find out how deep the cave went, she followed close behind.

Rathym led her to a large firepit with a spit. When he squatted down to blow fire into the embers, she noticed something hanging between his legs. He turned to retrieve something back the way he'd come, giving her a full, unfiltered view of his genitalia.

Genitalia, *plural.* Two thick, long appendages hung from his pelvis, with a huge set of balls underneath. Each were so large that they would shame the most well-hung porn stars she'd ever watched. The top one had a flared tip and prominent ridges all along its girth. The second was below and slightly to the right of the first, and was a smidge smaller. It was smooth and tapered to a gentle end.

Awestricken, Dana couldn't help but gape at them as he walked past. She hardly noticed him sneering at her.

"I refuse to abide by human decency, of which I neither subscribe nor condone." With that, he picked up his pace, cocks swaying with the quickened uptake of his stride.

Well, that's going to be very distracting. She cleared her throat and backpedaled to her bag, where she pulled out the eye drops and dropped some into both eyes. For some reason, she felt her eyes kept playing tricks on her lately.

Back in the dining room, Rathym set to work skinning and dressing the stag. She purposefully stared around the room, looking at anything but him. If she so much as peeked at his glistening scales or stared into his stunning double-iris eyeball, she was sure to accidentally look lower. Every gorgeous inch of him was alluring, but the corpulent, flaccid cocks were an entirely different kind of temptation. Her inner walls clenched at the mere thought of them. She busied herself with studying the piles of stuff everywhere, trying to figure out what made him place each of them in their spots.

Her explorations were short-lived. The cave was so massive she would have to walk for long stretches to pass from room to room, and her body was already sore. She wandered back to the dining room, which featured a long, polished table that could easily seat thirty or forty guests. Enchanting lamps with decorative colored glass cast a moody glow across the room. It looked like something straight out of a fairy tale. As long as she ignored the mounds of clutter in the adjoining rooms.

"So, where did most of this stuff come from?"

"I've collected treasures from all around the globe and all the known realms for centuries. My elven silver collection is rare and possibly the most coveted, as its species of origin has been…removed from existence. In fact, you remind me of a young princess I once knew."

"Really? What was she like?"

He chuckled fondly, but the sound chimed with sadness. "She was cunning and unyielding and always smilling. A great pain in my scales. Had she been given the chance, she would have grown into a great ruler."

"Oh. I'm so sorry."

He turned back to his task and added over his shoulder, "She was exceptionally beautiful and clever. You would have liked her. Everyone did."

That he found her comparable to a fae princess warmed her cheeks. It was especially complimentary coming from such a cultured and worldly man. Well, dragon.

"Your appreciation of the arts is lovely, but I'm confused. How can you be a kidnapper and still be so charming?"

Rathym grunted.

He presented her with an artfully arranged plate of herbal-scented meat and vegetables so beautiful it was suddenly easy to keep her eyes away from certain parts of his body. He took the seat across from her. His hulking form made the plates seem like petri dishes. He provided no utensils, and she realized quickly that he didn't use them—because why would he? He's a *dragon*.

"Tell me, human. How did you find yourself invading my lair?"

Dana snorted. "Invading? More like tumbling. I was pushed."

His stoic features hardened, his claw-tipped hand digging into the wooden table. "Elaborate."

"My boyf—my ex. He wants kids. I don't. He got tired of me denying him, I guess." She shrugged it off as though it wasn't a traumatizing event that would surely haunt her for the rest of her life. "I needed to end it with him anyway. But I felt obligated to stay after all he's done for me."

Dark clouds scuttled over his features, splintering his stoicism. His wings popped outward, growing in size. The crimson scales on his bare arms shimmered and

34

multiplied as his slitted nose pushed out into a snout. Then he shook himself, seeming to regain composure as all his features smoothed back down.

"The insignificant man dare not return to my domain," he growled. His intense gaze pinned her to her seat, the flecks of red in his extra iris alight. Heat blazed in her core and she felt the need to sit up straighter and slam her thighs together. "You are safe now, mortal. You will always be safe in our home."

The genuine compassion in his tone sent electricity sparking over her skin. She couldn't think of a response, even though she knew there was no way she could stay here. Was it bad that she was kind of *wanted* to? His reaction reminded her of the vindictive boyfriends in her favorite romance novels, and she got the distinct impression that he would truly gut Jackson if he ever set foot in this area.

The thought of this beast raining vengeance on her behalf made her whole body tingle, all the way from the back of her neck to her toes. She subconsciously glanced down at the table, which she knew hid two enormous cocks. She imagined being impaled on him while he spoke dirty words into her ear with his assertive voice. Heat warmed her cheeks when she realized where her mind had wandered.

As if he could smell her dirty thoughts, he dragged in a deep inhale before eating the meat from his plate in a way she could only describe as the epitome of carnal sensuality.

After their meal, Rathym nestled into the large bed

of blankets, transforming back into the fearsome dragon of legends. His tail wrapped around his large body mass and nestled under his chins. The sweet, kitten-like pose made her heart flutter. It was endearing. It made her chest ache with a pang of regret knowing what she must do the moment he fell asleep.

Even if she'd wanted to stay, what would be the point? There was no way he felt the same chemistry between them that she did. He called her things like *item, belonging, possession,* and lumped her in with the rest of the junk—albeit expensive and precious junk—that littered his cave.

Besides, so what if he did feel the chemistry between them? They would never, *could* never, *should* never be together in any meaningful way. He was an animal. Right? A great, mythological, magical beast. She was only human. By the looks of his...anatomy, they would never fit together sexually. It would be a sexless partnership, where one partner saw the other as a magnificent and out-of-league beast, and the other saw their partner as a pretty token.

It would never work.

Rathym's snores started out soft and gradually grew to fill the whole cave with rumbles that echoed one after another. She cast him one last rueful glance, the ache growing inside her chest.

Chapter 6
Rathym

Something was wrong.

Rathym woke to the feeling of danger deeply rooted in his bones. A threat. He erupted from dreaming ready to take on the threat to his home, only to find it utterly empty of trespassers.

Including his newest treasure.

The freshly scented trail she'd left behind drove him into the woods, where the pink hue of dawn bathed the forest ground. He pushed aside all fear for her safety. Centuries of service helped his composure to stay calm and alert. Battle ready. He spotted the pack of wolves before he saw what they were chasing, but he knew what he would find.

With an even dive, he beheaded the pack, taking out

the alpha with a crunch. The rest of the pack howled and whimpered, scattering into the trees like a headless snake slithering until its muscles gave way. But his hunt was not over. Where was his human?

The scent of her blood reached him along the tree line. He lifted one pair of eyes well above the trees, the other staying low so as not to lose her trail. His human was smart. She'd found a deserving hiding place.

But she could not hide from him.

There. At last, he found her trembling body compressed in a fox burrow. Without halting his wings, he downshifted and touched down a few feet away. The scent of her fear was stronger than ever, proof that she was capable of the emotion he had yet to smell from her so strongly. Careful not to spook her, he held his hands up and padded toward her.

"You are safe now, mortal," he said in a muted tone. "The wolves are gone. 'Tis only me, come to bring you home."

Her fear-stricken eyes shook as they landed on him, tears sparkling in her lashes. The delicate brown drops held the skittish look of small prey, but Rathym knew it did not belong there. She was a fierce and courageous one, albeit one who should not be meandering the woods alone.

"Y-y-you came for me."

"Of course." Did she think he wouldn't? "I don't allow harm to come to what is mine."

Something sparked in her fearful features as though she might push back, but she unfurled her arms from around her knees and extended a shaking hand. Rathym took it and helped her to stand. The moment she toddled upright, she fell into his arms.

"You're hurt."

Not allowing her time to resist, he scooped her into his arms and nestled her safely against his chest for the short flight home. Her fragrance was laced with fear. Rathym decided he didn't like the combination.

Once inside the cool walls of his cave, he laid Dana on the long table and examined her feet. Her right ankle was very swollen. He cursed himself for showing up too late. She was his responsibility. He was supposed to keep her safe, not allow her to be ambushed and overpowered. Once again, the ghosts of his past laughed and pointed fingers at his failure.

"This will need healing. Strip."

She balked and rose onto her hand, the elbow she'd been favoring held against her chest. Her face contorted with her usual argumentative nature. Rathym had little time for her falsely cheerful reasoning and began to prepare a healing salve.

"I'm fine. I don't need—"

"You do need!" he thundered. His temper took hold, enveloping him in a prickling warmth. In his peripheral, Dana flinched back. He took a steadying breath, but it hardly doused the flames. Smoke leaked from his nostrils. "How am I to keep you safe if you deceive me and run from me? I'm charged with your safety. Do not make me fail to protect you. This needs dressing, and I must assess you for further injuries."

"Rathym, I can't stay here." Her tone was pleading, but she removed her clothing like he'd asked. He ignored her and turned back to the salve.

"All of it," he commanded when he saw she'd left two strips of fabric in place. She obeyed.

The sight of her bare body lying on the table stoked the fire in his veins. She lay back and stared at the ceiling as he surveyed the damage, which was minor other than a large poorly-healed chunk of missing skin, presumably from her initial fall into his lair. He smeared the healing salve over the scabbed skin, eliciting a wince and a sharp inhale. As he traced her flesh farther down, his gaze flicked up to the stubble covering the sweet-smelling spot between her legs, the sign of a healthy and mature mate. The primal animal within him twitched to attention, his body desiring to fill his mate with buckets of seed until she was successfully bred. He licked his lips as the scent wafted down to meet his nostrils before returning to his work. Her swollen ankle was already bruising.

Rathym filled a goblet with wine from his enchanted bottle and slid it over to her. She gulped it down and held it out for more, which he obliged, which she promptly gulped down again. "Careful, human. This is not your typical wine."

"I can handle myself." She hiccupped and held the goblet out again.

Rathym's brow furrowed, but he grunted and obliged again. At least she would be safe here, should the dwarven drink knock her out.

"This will not feel pleasant," he warned.

All he wished to do right now was give her pleasure, if only to ensure she would never again run off to be ripped apart by wolves. He wanted to convince her she was better off here, with him, where she was safe and had all the comforts she could possibly need. Here, where nothing could harm her. But that was not the situation they found themselves in.

He rubbed the salve on her tender flesh with utmost care, treating her raw leg with the caress of a breeze and traveling down to her swollen ankle. To his surprise, the warm scent of her increased in intensity. A moan slipped from her lips. The toes on her other foot curled. The flame inside his bloodstream matched that of her stuttered breath. He glanced up to see her chin tilted back, eyes closed, plump lip caught in her teeth. He allowed his gaze to wander downward, drinking in her peaked nipples, which were hard and burnished like golden thimbles straight from the seamstresses of Elvendale.

He was supposed to be angry with her, but his body rebelled. The sight of her nearly writhing under his hands was too attractive to ignore. He wondered what sounds she would make if he massaged her in other places. Would she mewl like this? If she would make these perfect sounds from between his legs, then he wouldn't stop kneading her until her spark left her body under his touch.

The spell broke when she gasped in pain. He'd gotten careless. He backed away to clean up his work table, but he did not miss the glance she cast down at his half-stiff cocks before scrambling to cover herself.

Cursed flame! What the hells was he doing? The woman had drank three full goblets of dwarven wine, and here he was, imagining her thighs spread open below him. *Distance!* He must be more careful, but the damned faulty mate sensations were overwhelming, especially when she smelled and sounded so fucking *appetizing*.

"I'll bring you fresh clothing. Wait here." He flinched at his voice, which sounded like a creaky door hinge.

Deeper in the cave, where his softer, more sentimental items lived, he located the wardrobe that once belonged to Riniya, which she'd never grown old enough to wear. The flowing fabric would lie flatteringly against his human's slight curves, and it would bring him great joy to see a token of a long-ago friendship put to good use.

Among the items, he located a strip of fabric to wrap around his waist. The silky fabric was not too disruptive to his loins, and if it brought a modicum of comfort to his human treasure, then so be it. He could not allow her to be so repulsed by his form that she was moved to run away again. There were some ways he could compromise without abandoning his morals. She was more important than his pride. She was a transient and beautiful treasure, but moreover, she was a delicate species. A vulnerable human. Nearly anything could snuff her spark from the earth.

"Thank you," she said softly as she accepted the

dress. Then, hesitantly, she added, "Rathym?"

"Yes?"

"I'm sorry for causing you trouble." Her voice lowered until it was as quiet as the wind. When she spoke again, the words rushed out, like a gust rustling through cherry blossoms. "Are you upset with me?"

"It's no trouble, Dana," he assured her. Her glossy, downcast gaze briefly lifted to his. He extended a claw and raised her chin so she would see his earnesty. "I will always protect you. You belong here, with me."

She startled him by wrapping her arms around his waist, her bare chest pressing against the epidermal plates of his abdomen lusciously, sending both of his hearts beating in rapid succession. He recovered from his shock and clasped her firmly in place. When her warmth left him, he gently swiped the silken dress from her arm and draped it over her head, then scooped her up.

"Can you grab my bag? Need to take my contacts out."

"Yes. Lie down. I have pressing matters to attend."

"Aren't you worried I'll just leave again?"

Rathym huffed. "If your ankle does not deter you, this sleeping draught will. Though you drank enough dwarven alcohol to fell a small dragon."

He tucked her under the blankets and paused to brush a dark lock from her cheek. He stepped into a room tucked behind a tapestry, where his herbs and medicines were stored, and grabbed the potion labeled *Slumber*. Removing the cork, he flicked the vial twice into a mug of cold water and breathed fire against it enough to bring

43

the contents to lukewarm and refrain from melting the porcelain.

Dana accepted the mug and took a sip. Her eyes closed as she hummed in appreciation.

"I didn't know you had hot water down here. And what is in this tea? It's delicious!" She peered at him through eyes like little slits.

"It's an old herbal remedy. And all water can be easily warmed if you're Fireborn."

"So you really can breathe fire?" Her tone was filled with excitement, but a yawn trailed the end of her question. The draught was working quickly. Or was it the wine?

"Yes, I am gifted with the Great Flame." Rathym plucked the empty mug from her hand. He stumbled over his words when she lifted her arms in a broad stretch, her back arching from the bedding. He cleared his throat and turned away. "Enough elemental talk for now. Get your rest. I will return before you wake."

"Okay." The blankets rustled. "Hey, Rathym?"

"Yes?"

No answer. He set the mug down gently and turned around. The human was lying on her side, her petite frame tucked around itself, her mouth slightly ajar. She was rather exquisite like this, with sleep clinging to her and the only thing coming from her mouth the drool of slumber. It was fortunate that he must leave instead of giving in to his desire to curl his body around her. He couldn't pretend he hadn't felt the fire of his spark burn brighter when he'd carried her to bed.

But this could not be delayed, and he had a long flight. He'd waited centuries for this Ivaan Kovgroff to receive his reckoning. Perhaps something in those wretched parchments could explain why he'd had to wait so long.

Chapter 7
Rathym

The kingdom of the Great Flame had changed.

Rathym expected that to be the case, of course. Nothing stayed the same for two centuries. It was unsurprising to see the statues had changed, ancient dragons who'd fought for old ways of life replaced with dragons he didn't recognize. Empty lots now hosted buildings for various shops and eateries.

What he hadn't expected to see, however, was interspecies mingling everywhere he looked. He spotted dragons holding hands with minotaurs, harpies, and sirens. His homeland had apparently moved into the current century with more ease than he had. Not to mention he was one of few folks uncovered by some kind of loincloth or garment.

The council's headquarters remained in the same spot as always, much to Rathym's relief. He navigated the halls of the building by muscle memory. His feet took him straight to the head council member's door, which was closed. He rapped his knuckles on the door and heard shushing from the other side.

A short saffron dragon answered his knock. Over their shoulder, Rathym noticed three others in the room. Two dragons, and one elf. *An elf? In the council's quarters?* Curious.

"Sir Rathym Odrydimere!" The saffron dragon exclaimed his name as though they were old friends, but he didn't recognize the puny thing at all. "I—we are so glad you could make it. This is, after all, your accomplishment. Without your guidance, the old council would have dropped the case against—"

"Yes, I was there."

"Right, erm—"

"I've come to collect the paperwork on King Ludove's assassination."

"Ah! It should have been in the—"

"I haven't owned a ring in centuries," Rathym growled. His patience was growing thin. He glanced behind the council member and saw the room had cleared.

"Right, of course." The saffron dragon was now pale as a sheet. They stumbled backward into their office and waved at a figure behind a window. "Do come in. I apologize for my reaction. I was not expecting you so early. I am council member Kolloth, they/them, at your

47

service."

Rathym grunted. He didn't need to introduce himself. It was clear everyone had recognized him the moment the door was opened.

There was a soft rap on the door beside a window that peeked into an administrative office. The door opened a crack. A beautiful marigold dragon peered inside, waving a stack of parchment.

"Here's the—Rathym?"

"Anabraxus," he said around a lump in his throat. "You work for the council now?"

His childhood friend snorted. "That's what you ask me, after all these years? You stubborn old man."

He was about to retort when she closed the distance, embracing him with a ferocity he couldn't match. He accepted the affection through clenched teeth.

"Ryuu will be so happy to see you."

"I'm not staying."

Anabraxus stiffened. She pulled away and placed the folder on council member Kolloth's desk. "Of course not. But you'll return for the reckoning. If you'd like to see some friendly faces, my husband and I would love to have you. Come for dinner the night before."

When Rathym moved to speak, she held up a hand and turned away. "Think on it. You know where to find us."

As the door clicked closed behind her, the council member cleared their throat and extended the stack of parchment. A golden signet ring was perched on top of the paperwork.

"I would hate for you to have to come all this way again."

Rathym highly doubted there was anything else he wanted to discuss with the council, but he accepted the their offering and tromped out of the office, down the hall, down the staircase, and out the front door. He kept walking through the town square and didn't slow to observe the strange, unfamiliar setting of his homeland. He walked all the way to the edge of town before releasing his full form and taking to the skies.

He wasn't going home, not yet. He rose in the sky and traveled in the opposite way of his cave, not slowing until he saw the pool of shimmering molten orange sparkling below.

The air became thick, but not with heat. The heat did not affect him. The overwhelming pressure of grief, the humid fog of sorrow, affected him greatly. His claws dug into the viscous stream. He drew in a deep breath that did nothing to ease the ache in his chest.

The grieving lake was the resting place for all Fireborn, but Rathym also felt the presence of his dearest friends. Luvon was murdered by flames from a Fireborn, his whole body charred beyond recognition. In his hearts, Rathym knew the connection between the flames that killed him and the pool of magma meant a sliver of his spark went back to the Great Flame, which powered the grieving lake.

Little Princess Riniya's spark was somewhere within the churning depths as well. When the elves had fallen, their sacred resting place was destroyed. Rathym had returned to her palace too late to be useful. All he could do was excavate her body from the rubble and flee as the invading forces erected the barrier that would backfire, trapping everything within it in a distant, lifeless realm, only charred, rotten land left behind. He'd returned her spark to the lake of the Great Flame with the most painful tears he'd ever cried.

"Luvon." His tongue was so heavy, the strength it took to form words was exhausting. "Luvon. Riniya." A sob tore from his throat, thick with ash and pain. "I thought it would feel better than this."

He fell into the pool. The sparkling stream was warm on his legs. With every heave of his shoulders and every rumbling cry that forced its way from his chest, he felt his burden lighten. Luvon and Riniya were with him, their sparks glistening orange embers behind his eyelids.

There was so much more to say, but his whole body revolted when he tried to speak. He curled up in the burning churn of magma and remained there, overtaken by grief, until their sparks returned to the depths.

With a sobering sense of calm, Rathym pulled himself together for the long trip home.

Home. Where a warm, human body slumbered in his bed.

Rathym returned to the comfort of his new home

right in time for his midday nap. Unfortunately, there was the matter of the paperwork that scorched in his hands.

The largest chunk of parchment rambled on about nothing. For years, they'd had only one detective working the case. Why was he not surprised? Nothing useful was reported until 156 years in, which was also when the claw print of the detective's superior changed.

In the following years, the lone detective became part of a team. One member of that team was transferred from Species Relations, whose notes were adamant that Ivaan Kovgroff was a main suspect based on his known connection to the dark fae who'd accompanied the charlatan human usurper.

Known connection?

Rathym bristled. How had they not caught him right then and there? Instead, they dicked around for another century or so. When they finally got him, there were more charges added to his rap sheet, including *complicity to genocide* and *conspiracy to genocide* and *obstruction of justice to an ally*.

Heat filled Rathym's throat. He'd never considered that the two crimes were connected. Why had he not seen it before? Was he just as blind as the detective had been?

He tossed the paperwork on the table and seethed. His blood boiled. Smoke and flame leaked from his snout.

He wasn't sure how long he paced, but at last he felt his fury simmer. He only hoped he hadn't woken Dana. Her body needed rest. She would likely sleep on through the night thanks to the draught.

It was evening now. Too early to go to bed, but he'd missed his nap anyway. His bones were weary with the kind of exhaustion that came from renewed grief. His mind was muddled, his hearts in tangles. The strength required to keep his distance from the treasure in his bed was not something he possessed. With the human's warmth against his scales, he nuzzled into her neck and rumbled a deep, masculine purr involuntarily. Hair the dark, rich color of a sturdy chestnut tree in its prime tickled his snout.

When the sharp blossom of emotion that only belonged between mates bloomed inside of him, he didn't fight it. It was much better than the burning heat of revenge or the sting of guilt. He allowed the peculiar emotion to carry him into a place between sleep and wakefulness, where he felt a deep companionship, as if he'd never lost his home. As if it were right here all along.

An intrusive thought pierced his drowsing mind. Could it be that he, a centuries-old, mature, and experienced dragon, hosted resentment toward the human species under false pretenses? Was it possible he was even *jealous* of their open affection and kinship, his bitterness but a result of his own loneliness? Yes, one sour human and their fae-enhanced army had committed genocide, but not all humans were charlatans. If his homeland had embraced interspecies relations, why did he still feel ambivalent?

Why did it feel impossible to pry open his heart?

Chapter 8
Dana

Dana slept like a baby, her dreams pleasant and warm. When she woke, she felt the warm imprint of scales where Rathym cradled her. Had he stayed with her all night?

Wait. When had she gone to bed? *His* bed?

Blurry images formed behind her eyelids. Staring at the ceiling of the cave, lain bare on the dining table. The ceiling starting to swirl as adept claw-tipped hands roamed her lower body. Rathym's two hardening lengths as he backed away. The anxiety she always felt when she thought someone was unhappy with her. His chest scales, somehow both hard and soft, pressed against her breasts. Snuggled in the blankets, the desire to coax him to lay down with her dying on her lips.

Oh, fuck. He could have easily taken advantage of her. Here she was, protectively tucked against him, and she wholeheartedly believed he would never harm her.

Aside from the headache that was assuredly caused by the weird-tasting wine, her whole body ached. Her muscles were sore from the full-body wracking she'd done while hiding from the pack of wolves. Though it seemed impossible, she swore she could feel the healing lotion working to knit her skin and muscle back together.

Not wanting to burst the cocoon around them, she held completely still and ignored the signals from her body for a while. The electric circuit between their skin made her heart pitter-patter like rain on a reading nook window, little lightning bolts skittering across her skin. Soon, the aches in her body won and she shifted.

"Good morning, my treasure."

Oh god, is that my new nickname? She sure hoped so. In his deep, gravelly drawl, heavy with sleep, it was all he had to say to make her core flutter to attention. She bit her lip to restrain a giggle at the silly flip-flopping going on in her abdomen.

"Good morning." She hesitated before reaching out to cup his cheek. The scales on his face were smoother than those on his arms and back. She stroked her thumb over them as he leaned more weight into her palm. "Sorry I woke you."

"How are you feeling? You slept a long time. Do you feel rested?"

"A teensy bit sore, but much better than I *should* be feeling. Whatever's in that mixture is definitely helping

54

my ankle." The gleam in his eye coupled with a slight smirk made her pause. "What? What's in that cream?"

Rathym extracted himself from the bed and produced the healing lotion. He slathered a healthy amount on her ankle with more formality than the intimate encounter the night prior, but his skillful hands felt amazing all the same.

Content with his inspection, he began about his morning. The routine seemed lived-in and natural, and Dana found herself wondering what it would be like to share a normal, daily routine with him. The thought warmed her insides. She considered him further and realized he was still in his condensed form and had been sporting a long, front-and-back draped loincloth ever since he'd rescued her.

"The salve is a compound of magical elements, including medicinal herbs, scales, and seed."

She startled at his voice, having long forgotten she'd asked about the healing salve as she'd become lost in her daydreams.

"Like, poppy seed?"

"No." He peered at her darkly over his shoulder, a predatory grin tugging at one side of his crimson mouth. "My own."

"Oh. *Oh!*"

The warmth in her cheeks spread until her ears were burning, and yet something tickled between her legs. It wasn't exactly sexy, but thinking of it in that context very quickly led her to consider another context where she would be covered in his *seed*. She squeezed her thighs together, hoping his sensitive ears didn't pick up on the flood of liquid.

Rathym's nostrils flared and she knew it was no use. Even if he hadn't heard the sudden trickle, he certainly smelled it. *Why bother?* She held her head a little higher. Let him know she wanted him. What did it matter? She couldn't hide it anyway.

With a sigh, she hauled herself off the bedding, favoring her weak ankle heavily. Slowly but surely, she reached her bag and dug for her phone.

"Shit."

No service. What did she expect? *I guess that collections job wasn't meant to be.* Unsurprising and a bit of a relief, actually. Would the temp agency accept her back for another assignment if she no-showed the first job they gave her?

"What troubles you?" Rathym's extremely deep voice reverberated against the stone walls. He must've changed into his full form.

She tucked the phone back in her bag and followed the sound of his voice to the dining room, their plates out of place on the obscenely long table. One of his tree-trunk-sized necks curved to look at her, the other still focused on the bloody task in front of him. The sight of so much blood made her queasy, so she focused solely his red-hued irises as they watched her behind filmy horizontal-sliding eyelids.

"I was supposed to start work this morning. They probably won't want me now."

"Why would you need to work?" His words

slithered off his long, forked tongue. This version of him sounded significantly different, yet still entrancing.

"I need a job. How else would I make money?"

The bumped ridge of muscle over his eye drew down. "Whatever would you need money for?"

"You know. Stuff." Dana rolled her eyes and gestured helplessly. "Everything costs money! Rent. Food. Wi-Fi."

His other head glanced back at her, all four of his brows deeply furrowed. "But we have all we need."

Her jaw dropped open to retort, but no sensible argument came out. Technically, he was right. He'd prepared tasty dishes using only herbs and animals from the forest for each meal. He'd adorned her in clothes too beautiful for her lower-middle-class status.

"Well, Wi-Fi then," she ceded with a shrug, although even that wasn't totally necessary. She'd rather enjoyed not being glued to her social media the past day and a half. "I do have to talk to my family somehow."

This he seemed to understand. His head retreated and his body morphed into the smaller reptilian version, which she assumed was more practical for things like cooking and really anything that required opposable thumbs, but he managed to do a lot of things in both forms. He retrieved the blue-and-gold embroidered loincloth, which had obviously been made from the same fancy elven material as her dress and looked like it had belonged to a warrior. He turned away as he draped it over himself.

"Why don't you stay in this form?"

"It isn't sustainable to remain in downshift for long stretches. I spent the night with you like this. This morning it's causing minor discomfort." He breathed fire into the pit.

"I'm sorry. I didn't mean to cause you pain."

"No. I wanted to. It was…it was nice."

Dana's cheeks warmed. A shy smile caused her to dip her chin, but she made herself meet his gaze. "It was. Nice, I mean."

"What would you do, if you did not think you needed coin?"

The answer came to her immediately. "Write. I write fantasy romance books. I mean, I used to. My readers have probably all forgotten about me."

He hummed contemplatively and then held up a claw-tipped finger. He disappeared into some hidden nook of the seemingly endless cave. When he returned, he placed a typewriter in front of her, along with some frayed parchment, a quill, and a small container of black ink.

"The ink is enchanted to never spill nor go dry, and the contraption is charmed with an endless scroll of parchment." He grinned smugly, his broad shoulders high, his arms crossed over his chest. "There. Now you want for nothing."

A swell of gratitude threatened to burst from Dana's chest. She'd never received such a thoughtful gift, and this man—dragon—had only known her for days, and yet here he was, lavishing her with gifts and calling her his treasure. She felt *seen*. Like for once, she didn't have to prove herself worthy of someone's attention.

"What is it now?" he asked, his caring expression souring. "You still wish to leave?"

"No!" she responded too quickly. Belatedly, she realized what she'd said. In the millisecond after, she also realized how true it was. Where would she go, anyway? Back to shrinking herself for the benefit of others? "No. I don't want to leave. This is perfect. I've never—I don't know what to say, Rathym."

She kneeled on the chair and leaned over the table to place a hand on his arm. "Thank you."

His smug grin returned. A forked tongue slipped from his mouth. "Anything for you, my treasure."

The pet name sent a hot thrill through her core. She watched his eyes trail down to her lips. They continued down her body until the slightest flare of his nostrils gave away that he was searching for the scent of her desire. She suppressed a sly smile and leaned back in her chair. The people-pleaser inside her cowered, knowing that what she was about to say would ruin the moment.

"I'll still need to contact my family at some point, though," she reminded him gently.

The bubble popped instantly. He gave a stiff nod and returned to the food, leaving Dana to mourn the loss of his sweet side. She drank in the sight of his broad back, which was covered in an array of red-hued scales from dusty pink to bright crimson. She wondered about the loincloth. He'd specifically stated that he wouldn't play by the rules of *human decency*. What made him change his mind? Was it due to her reaction to him, or some unexpected desire to be modest? She highly doubted it was the latter and couldn't help feeling guilty for causing him to think he had to cover himself in his own home. Plus, she rather missed seeing all of him at once. At least the slip of fabric did keep her thoughts tame.

She turned her focus to the enchanted writing supplies and wondered what to write about. The idea came rather quickly. She jotted down a few sentences of a summary—the most outlining anyone would ever catch her doing—and set off.

Time passed by unnaturally in the cave. It was surreal, bizarre, like the fog that grows inside the mind while on an extended vacation, and didn't she deserve a break?

With the strange passing of time, she could have spent days or hours at the typewriter, her writing slump shattered. Between the sharp pain of her leg and the dreamlike haze, she rarely rose from the chair unless she had to use the primitive toilet. Dana typed ceaselessly while Rathym cooked, brooded, and watched her.

The only telltale signs that days were passing were the five-star meals. In the mornings, he served her breakfast, then retreated to the bed and shed his reptilian form. An hour or so later, he would return, just to sit in comfortable silence save for the sound of the keys.

After lunch, like clockwork, the cave was filled with the loud snores of two enormous dragon heads. At times, it was frustrating to write with so much noise, but she couldn't help laughing to herself. Even as a huge, formidable dragon, her companion was strangely human. Not human-human, but more like, he was *understandable*. His presence was easy, warm, even when he was curt or quiet. She got the sense that he was hiding from something. Like there was a deeper reason he'd secluded himself in this cave.

When he woke from his nap, he went hunting. He always returned with meat to cook into dishes like stew, roast, steak. All of his recipes made her taste buds dance. Whatever spice blends he used, they were nothing she'd seen in the grocery store before. They ate dinner together every night. Dana would swoon over the tasty food, and Rathym would grin smugly, pride and arrogance swimming in his double irises.

Every night, they snuggled in the blankets. By morning, she always awoke under his full-sized claw.

It was like she was living a daydream, her real life far away, the good girl she'd always been long forgotten.

On this day, her fingers click-clacked on the long-unused keys. It was a satisfying sound that brought forth childhood memories. When her grandmother was alive, Dana and her mom would fly to Indonesia to visit. Dana would spend hours in the cozy study-slash-writing nook that smelled like old books, where her gran always had fresh paper waiting for her.

Dana loved those visits. Her eyes prickled at the memory. She gulped down a sudden lump in her throat and shook her head. She smiled at the thought of her gran seeing her now, shacked up with a dragon and an enchanted typewriter. She could almost hear her say the equivalent of, *Good riddance to what anyone else thinks. You know what's in your heart.*

Sometime midday, her wrists began to cramp and her eyesight became unreliably foggy. Who knew typewriters were so far from ergonomic? She stood and pushed her fists into her lower back, then stretched her arms high. Rathym walked in with a bundle of clothing and some towels.

"You really have a bath?" She sniffed her armpit and crinkled her nose. "You should've said something sooner!"

"I'm not a monster. I bathe. Come."

With a giddy grin, she followed him a little too quickly, sending a sharp pain through her mostly healed ankle. She winced and walked more carefully. The healing salve was doing wonders that defied modern medicine. Her scraped leg was basically healed and her twisted ankle only hurt when she walked too hastily. She grew confused when he directed her to the uphill tunnel that led outside. Before she could react, he swooped her into his arms and exited the cave.

They emerged from the hidden passageway and immediately took to the air. Rathym's wings redirected the air with powerful gusts, shimmering in the high sun. When Dana was able to tear her attention from his beauty, she was rewarded with the awe-inspiring sight below. The vast, lush nature playground was way better from this angle than any summit she'd ever accomplished. His scarlet chromatic wings beat around her like a second heart, their twinkling trails casting the air around him into a rosy hue.

Not long ago, she'd known for a fact that dragons didn't exist. She'd thought her polite life with Jackson was as good as it would get. That she was lucky even, just for having someone willing to pay the bills while she followed her dream.

Now here she was, soaring above the trees in the arms of a centuries-old mythical beast, who she was finding herself more and more enamored with. Somewhere between that fateful fall to her death and this moment, Rathym had begun to carve out a dragon-sized space in her heart.

Surrounded by the carmine beat of his wings, she felt free.

Chapter 9
Dana

After a few minutes of flying, they came upon a waterfall. With the grace of a being centuries old, Rathym glided down and gently placed Dana's feet on the ground. Dana could feel his gaze on her as she took in the enchanting sight.

The waterfall emptied into a basin of crystal-clear water. The ground was speckled with smooth pebbles of all colors. Bright green moss grew in the cracks and on the mounds that surrounded the spring. Rathym approached the waterfall and stepped through. He breathed fire on a perfectly paved shelf-like semi-circle behind the flowing water, creating steam.

It was a scene pulled straight from a fantasy novel.

"Wow," she whispered breathlessly. She didn't

hesitate to disrobe. He'd already seen her naked on the table. This setting would at least be more flattering.

Rathym not-so-subtly watched her with his signature expression bordering on arrogance. She could practically see him add a tally to his balance toward *keeping her here.* Little did he know, Dana was keeping track of her own skewed version of the same tally, and this ticked another point toward *leaving society to live with a super old dragon.*

The toasty water was glorious. She closed her eyes and reclined weightlessly, using only her arms in little circles to stay afloat. With a contented sigh, she let her uninjured leg drift underneath her and stood on the tip of her toes. It wasn't too deep that she couldn't touch, and having the weight off her ankle felt almost as helpful as the healing solvent.

Rathym bathed nearby, no longer hiding his glances in her direction. Her view of his body was obstructed by a mound of rock, but the fire in his eyes and smoke billowing from his nostrils told her all she needed to know.

The flame in his double irises gave her an idea. She'd never been fond of the spotlight, but throughout their time together, he'd seemed to only have eyes for her anyway. Besides, the tension between them would have to give way at some point, right? Regardless that her bullies—and her sister—teased her for being a goody-two-shoes, she'd never been afraid to make the first move. But something about his being a totally different species made her hesitate. Could a dragon develop true feelings for a human? What if it was all in her mind and he'd only thought of her as a pet all along?

What if their companionable silence was like the quiet affection between a house cat and their owner?

That was the thought that kept her from taking action. She needed him to make the first advance to avoid making a fool of herself.

But that didn't mean she had to make it easy for him to resist.

Embodying the most fierce Beyoncé version of herself, she lay back and swam tits-up toward the flowing stream. She wished her breasts were more voluptuous, but she'd been gifted a flat chest and a spindly, bony body, all knees and elbows. Still, she felt his eyes on her even behind her eyelids.

When she reached the gentle thunder of the waterfall, the balmy air constricted her breathing a little. Her contacts didn't love the situation, but she ignored them. She rose from the water in a manner she hoped was sultry despite her ankle. In her peripheral, she could see she'd captured his attention. *Good.*

She proceeded to half-wash, half-dance in the steamy water. She felt a little silly—okay, a lot silly—but she was empowered by the way his stare became more and more lustful. She let her thumbs graze her nipples as she directed the warm water down to trace her swaying hips. She called to mind the old pin-up ladies and how they made men swoon just by pulling up their stockings. Slowly and with great, sensual care, she mimicked the image in her mind's eye, bending at the waist, letting one knee drift crooked. Shifting her weight with another swish of her hips, she straightened, allowing her head to tilt back. She ran her fingers through her hair, holding her arms just so, then dropped them back to her body to follow the rivulets of water down the expanse of her stomach, all the way to the apex of her thighs.

A loud splash came from Rathym's corner. She glanced up to see two sets of eyes, all four rapt on her body. His full form took up all the space on the pebbled beach, even flattening some trees with his rump. A forked tongue hissed out of the leftmost head, the sound not seeming entirely voluntary.

Did he lose control over me? She hoped so. She'd witnessed him nearly lose hold of his *downshift* once before, when she'd told him how she'd wound up in his cave.

She stared down the enormous two-headed creature, hoping to convey that she was not afraid of him. Not put off by him. Even though the massive beast was painted as an antagonist in so many fairy tales, she welcomed his fiery gaze. *Craved* it. The flare of all his nostrils told her he could smell the liquid heat growing between her legs. The sparks between their locked eyes might as well have been a visible string for how intensely she felt it, like a strike of lightning that could cut her down here and now if only he reached out and traced her skin with one of his sharp claws.

A mindless shift of her weight made her ankle throb. She winced before she could stop herself, but it was too late. Rathym was already downshifted and rushing toward her before she caught her next breath.

Before he scooped her into his arms, she was rewarded with a full view of the arousal she'd caused. Her eyes widened, her lips curved upward, and her body ached with need.

Too soon, he set her down on the bank and retrieved his scrap of cloth. Oh, well. At least she knew her little scheme had hit its mark. Maybe he would act on it soon. Maybe he would quell the hollow ache inside her, the desperate need to be filled to capacity, to be impaled on one or *both* of his cocks.

Her thoughts turned a little bitter as she realized her scheme had not only worked on him, but had also deeply frustrated herself.

"When we return, you will read me your story."

"What? No way!"

All the residual heat drained at that one sentence. Her neck snapped toward him so quickly it hurt. She would never let someone see her first draft! First drafts were not for viewing. But Rathym didn't bother arguing and she knew she'd lost already. Whenever he used that authoritative, commanding, *sexy* tone, she knew she was hopeless to disagree.

When they got home—*when did it start to feel like home?*—he pointed at her seat and started on dinner.

"Read."

Oh, god.

With a sigh and a long-winded disclaimer about not having written in a while, Dana plopped into the chair.

"Seriously, it won't even read the same once it's done. You're way better off waiting for the final product!" she huffed one last time before launching into the story.

The story was about a human detective and her dragon partner, a crime-solving duo who were the top of their line. In the middle of solving a murder mystery, the woman realized there was a connection between her and her partner that she hadn't seen before.

As she read, her cheeks became red-hot. Obviously, she'd known the dragon part was inspired by her current roommate, but how had so much of herself seeped into this story? Dana squirmed in her chair, her arm hair rising, her eyes glancing up at Rathym's stoic mask every few words. She felt raw, more bare than she'd been while standing naked in the steamy waterfall. More vulnerable than when she'd lain naked on the table.

Although his expression was devoid of any clues, she still felt his gaze scalding her just as it had in the spring.

"That's all I've got so far." She cleared her throat. "What do you think?"

"I find myself partial to Ramona and hope she will accept a dragon mate." He stared at his untouched plate thoughtfully. His ochre-and-crimson irises snapped to hers. "You'll continue to read me your progress over dinner. I must know how it ends, and if Ramona will accept his advances."

His seriousness made her giggle, which transformed his frown into a glower.

"Okay, okay. I'll read it to you every night."

After dinner, they naturally navigated to the large smattering of blankets, where she rustled through her bag to remove her contacts. Rathym thoroughly inspected and medicated her ankle with his special cream. Then he brought her a teacup that smelled of spice, definitely different than the one he'd given her to help her sleep. She eyed it warily.

"It's not more of your—erm—seed, is it?"

Rathym's rumbling laughter caught her off guard. It sounded as rough as a gemstone chipped straight from the earth, like it was the first time he'd laughed in years. Like it had taken him by surprise as well.

"No. Merely a blend of spices meant to assist a speedy recovery. Your little *stunt* may have upset the healing process."

She rolled her eyes. Of course he would think of that. Always hyper-aware of her safety.

Between the day's excursion and her body reserving its energy for healing, Dana was exhausted. She leaned into his warm presence, his two heartbeats thumping rhythmically against her back, his scaled arm draped over her protectively.

As she hovered at the precipice of sleep, she felt him shift. The weight of his arm on her waist turned into a large claw that covered her body, cradling her, easing her into a comfortable sleep.

Chapter 10
Rathym

The rise and fall of his human's petite chest brought a sense of comfort he hadn't known he was lacking. In her presence, Rathym's could take a deep, invigorating inhale, relaxing into a state of contentment. Even her silence was beautiful, a balm to his spark.

He surveyed the room around them, wall to ceiling with riches. He scanned for an item that could possibly measure up to the admiration he felt for the treasure under his claw.

There was nothing. No item, no matter how valuable, could possibly hold a match to the inferno Dana lit within him. The blaze roared inside him constantly, begging to be set free, to turn into a destructive wildfire. Unbearable, undeniable heat, like the lava pit of his homeland, lived within his very core. Too hot for a mortal to withstand.

A dragon and human pairing was inconceivable. He would not have deigned to consider it mere weeks ago. Improper. Dishonorable. Foolish. But the woman under his claw had changed his mind on many things. Between her and his unrecognizable homeland, he now saw the truth: he was nothing but a resentful old man who needed to change. He would've never considered that possibility if she hadn't fallen into his lair.

What scared him now was not that she would deny him, but that she would inevitably leave his side. He no longer possessed the cruel grit necessary to keep her against her will. It was true that he didn't like his beloved things strewn about, but with her, it went beyond that. Even if her feelings were true, she still possessed a delicate human body. What if something happened, and he wasn't quick enough to reach her? The spark of a human was easily snuffed out. Every day, humans died for seemingly no reason, dropping dead in the street or never waking from their bed.

Dana rustled against his palm. He downshifted to greet her, his lower half bare from sleeping in his full form and acutely aware of every brush of her skin. She stretched, her toes tickling his scales. Her slender frame arched against him, and he could not tear his hungry gaze from her body, the masterful work of art that was his greatest treasure.

"Good morning." Her voice was husky with sleep. Her golden-brown eyes met his and she reached a dainty hand to cup his cheek.

All night, his mind had been filled with thoughts of only her, considering and discarding schemes to keep her in his life. Even his dreams were filled with his treasure's luxurious sounds, movements, and touches. He leaned into her palm and wrapped an arm around her back to press her body against his. A little whimper escaped her ample lips, and he licked his own, his gaze locked on her mouth. He heard and felt her heart speed up, her gaze as defiant and undaunted as ever.

He dipped his chin without meaning to. Their lips met in a hesitant caress. He wanted to devour her, but he longed to do so slowly, so he took his time and pressed sweet kisses against her lips until she blossomed open. He pressed into her mouth with his forked tongue and greedily swallowed her sweet little whimpers. Her knees tightened together, the strong fragrance of her arousal singing to him from between her thighs.

Rathym retreated, enjoying the way she chased after him. But he wouldn't rush. He wanted to worship her, but first he had to address his concerns.

"I am much older than you, my treasure. Compared to your lifespan, I am ancient." He watched for her reaction.

"I've never met someone so worldly."

"My age does not bother you?" He squinted. She shook her head, her hand warm on his cheek. Her thumb swirled over the patch of scales under his eye. "I will have…difficulty when you are away."

"I'll always return."

"Downshifting is not sustainable. You will spend a significant amount of time with a fully matured dragon."

"Both of your forms are perfect the way they are."

"Your answers please me." He kissed her forehead and pulled her against his chest. "How are you able to see the good in everything?"

She was quiet for a few moments. When she spoke again, her breath was warm against his soft underbelly. "My mom came to America for college and wound up staying. She tried to convince my grandma, but she wouldn't leave her home. When I was little and visited her, I saw how different things could be, all balanced on *one* decision. I don't want to take anything for granted. There's more to life than what we find ourselves attached to. Everything is always changing. I just go with the flow."

"I've grown very fond of you, my treasure. I will always keep you safe."

"I know."

"I was wrong before." He nuzzled his broad snout against her neck. "We belong together."

Suddenly she was too far away. He needed her closer. Needed her all around him, below him, on top of him.

He placed the little container she used to store her sight enhancements in front of her. Once she was done, he nudged her down.

"You must be sore. Lie on your belly and I will massage your weary body."

As she obeyed, he lifted the loose fabric from her

legs and pushed it up to her shoulders. She squirmed to remove it altogether. He trailed his gaze hungrily over her curves, tracing the dip of her hips and the rise of her buttocks with his claw. The gasp and the trail of goose flesh his touch elicited sent a current of desire straight to his cocks, which twitched to attention. He wanted to grasp one in his hand to relieve the pressure, but he refused to turn a single sliver of his attention away from his treasure.

He kneeled beside her and kneaded her back and shoulders with his fists. Her breathy moans unleashed a torrential storm of primal desire that drove him to straddle her backside. He attempted to tilt his hips away so as not to invade her with his increasingly hardening lengths. He worked his way down, kneading and rubbing, until he reached her buttocks and hips. This spot was a particularly sore muscle for females, and so he kneaded with fervor, relishing the moans his touch elicited. He couldn't help but wonder if those moans would sound similar if he were to massage her from the inside.

Unable to stop himself, he grabbed two perfectly round fistfuls of her cheeks and squeezed, watching the way her skin pulled apart at the seam to reveal two perfectly placed entrances. His treasure moaned even for this kind of touch, her back arching, moving the incredible sight closer to his rapt eyes and drooling mouth. Again he struggled with the urge to reach away and stroke himself, or to lower his head and press his long tongue along that seam, to swirl it inside of each entry just to taste the hidden treasures inside.

The part of himself that recognized her as his mate loudly commanded him to take her right now, to shove himself inside her petite cunt and spray her womb with his seed, only backing out to slam inside with his second cock and fill her with more.

With great difficulty, he continued down her thighs and showed cautious care to her injured leg. Then he climbed back up, kneading and working her muscles. When he reached her lower back and continued to rise, his top cock rubbed against the scorching liquid heat that coated her slightly stubbled folds. At this sensitive touch, he growled under his breath, warm smoke leaking through his teeth. Dana squeezed and lifted her hips, rubbing the balmy heat against his upper shaft and locking both his cocks between her thighs.

She repeated the motion, up and down, and on the next upward lift she pressed against his cock hard enough that her cunt blossomed open, spreading even more searing slickness along his shaft. Their moans mingled as she repeated the motion with a hint of desperation, her blessed nectar coating his cock with slippery juices. Rathym swallowed the smoke pooling in his mouth.

He allowed her to continue creating the friction she craved as he massaged her shoulders. When his cock was doused with slickness, he reached down and lifted it, settling it between the seam of her ass. He held it there with one hand as she restarted the rise and fall, wetting his bottom shaft from base to tip.

"You are going to make me lose control," he warned. The fire in his throat bubbled like a boiling pot of stew, little puffs of smoke swirling from his nostrils. He was barely maintaining his downshift.

His warning only seemed to encourage her. He retreated a little in attempt to refocus on the guise of a massage, but she leaned up on her toes and tilted her hips just so. She was so wet and needy that the innocuous motion captured the tip of his bottom cock, nearly sucking him right inside of her dripping cunt. The walls of her tight hole strangled his cock, her tiny human pussy resistant to let him in.

Her startled cry held both pleasure and pain. Rathym slipped out of her and smacked her ass in reprimand.

"If you aren't good, you'll have to take these cocks before your body is ready," he growled. "You'll get yourself hurt that way."

His treasure, ever defiant and oh so brave, rolled onto her side. She captured his cocks between her saturated thighs. Her gaze locked on his as she rocked her hips, her moist skin slipping over him deliciously. The gentle caress tugged at his tenuous control, but when he looked into her dauntless golden stare, he saw right through her ruse.

It was a dare.

A primal sound escaped his throat. The sound pierced his treasure's thin veil of bravery, a flicker of her deeper need flashing across her beautiful features.

"You are not prepared for me."

She might be determined, but she would not coerce

him with false bravado. She didn't know who she was dealing with. He would shatter her as many times as it took, and then he would let the fragments stitch together just to destroy her again.

He would ruin her for any other man or beast.

Chapter 11
Dana

*D*ana had never felt so needy.

She wanted him. *Bad.* If that meant she had to play dirty, so be it. The ache in her core was begging to be filled, but instead of falling to her knees to plead that he ease her emptiness, she stared him down.

Dana was not delusional. She knew she was at least pretty, her burnished bronze skin a gift from her heritage, her piercing brown stare among her favorite features. Even as she'd suffered through high school and into young adulthood with body image and friends who didn't understand her whatsoever, she'd known she was desirable. But this assertive, brooding, sexy old dragon tested her.

His little interrogation proved he cared for her more

than a pet, and his two colossal cocks were steel-straight with desire for her. So why did he hold back?

You are not prepared for me.

The feeling of his two thick cocks between her legs proved his words were likely correct. The sheer length of them was difficult to comprehend, at least twice as large as any human man she'd been with. The width was exaggerated, too. Not to mention the *ridges*. Little circular ribs of raised skin lined his top cock, while the bottom cock was smooth, with a tapered head. When she'd managed to sneak the tip of it inside her, the sparks of pain were louder than the pleasure. Still, she longed for him to sink into her completely, *needed* it more than anything she'd ever needed before.

His tail flicked beside her. Covered in the same soft reptilian skin as his stomach, the tip came to an angled end with ribbed edges only along the underside. It was within reach. She plucked it off the blanket and brought it to her mouth, licking the raised red lines, testing the roughness. The rubber-like texture wasn't painful against her tongue. The thickness was less intimidating than his cocks and fit into her mouth without a problem. She swirled her tongue around the tip, flicking over the little ridges, then bobbed her head and suctioned her cheeks. The appendage twitched in the back of her throat. The surprising sensation made her moan involuntarily, subconsciously picking up the pace of her wiggling on his cocks, her clit nearly burning with need.

When the wave of excitement died down, she opened her eyes and locked onto his. In all three of his pupils shone a mirror of her own carnal desire, the glaze of lust mixed with a growing sense of urgency. She sucked his tail farther into her mouth until it hit the back of her throat, and then pushed it farther. Rathym growled and reached between her thighs to grip his top cock and tug with an odd look in his eyes, like he'd just lost an argument with himself.

She pushed his tail farther, farther, breathing carefully through her nose. As she deepthroated his tail, she saw his gaze drop to her neck. She wondered if he could see a bump there. Wondered if her stomach would swell with him, too. She pulled it out and took a gasp of air before starting the process again.

At last, she watched his resolve crumble. Plumes of smoke puffed from his nostrils. When his forked tongue flicked out to wet his lips, little embers sizzled between his teeth.

He lifted her from the bed and carried her to a tall golden surface. It must have been made for some kind of giant because it was tall enough that he stood between her dangling knees, stroking his cocks in his hand as he dangled his tail in front of her, arrogantly smirking when she chased it with her open mouth.

"Is this what you want?" He kept his tail, still glistening with her saliva, just out of reach. "Something to suck on while I make you come around my tongue?"

Her empty walls fluttered and clutched around nothing, the sound of his domineering voice making her body move of its own accord. She arched her back and whimpered as he stroked her cheek with the ribbed edges but pulled out of her reach when she turned to capture it.

"Answer me."

"Y-yes. Please. Give me something to suck on."

He chuckled darkly. The tip of his tail traced her throat, her jaw, her cheek, then met her lips with a caress gentle enough to be a kiss. She moaned and opened her mouth for him, glad to have something, *anything*, of his inside of her.

Claws teased her skin from hips to knees. He pulled her thighs wider, revealing every inch of her to his hungry gaze, like he was just sitting down for a meal of his favorite dish. She felt her folds part, ready for something to slide inside, to fill her, to thrust away at the aching emptiness in her core.

He pressed gentle kisses to the sensitive skin of her inner thighs, all the way up to the spot where her thighs met, where she needed him most. She whined around his tail as he skipped past her pussy to kiss and lick down the other leg. When he finally returned to her slick folds, she was so needy that she was rolling her hips over the table.

His long, forked tongue stroked her slick seam, parting it all the way. Although she'd seen bright patches of burning embers in his mouth, there was no red-hot pain. She moaned and quickened the pace on his tail, glad for the distraction from her growing disparity. His tongue traced her slickness again, this time flicking her clit, sending shivers through her whole body. She freed her mouth from his tail to say his name, her knees quivering.

"I did not say you could stop."

When he spoke, his claw-tippcd fingernails became searing hot, pressing into her hips until she obeyed. She set a steady pace with her sucking and licking, if only to make him return his tongue to her.

This time, his tongue dipped inside her. The surprising length of it reached inside her cunt and curved, flicking and swirling inside as though he were sampling every crevice. She didn't dare stop sucking his tail, not willing to risk his retreat, so she moaned around the mouthful. Rathym matched her with a groan, the vibrations of which reverberated straight to her core, a ripple effect that left her with goose bumps. As he explored her insides, he brought his thumb to her clit and circled it with just the right amount of pressure.

She mumbled incoherently. Her vision went black. She dropped his tail, her hands flying to his horns, clinging desperately. Her breath stuttered, the wave of her orgasm an unstoppable force. The knot inside her stomach burst into a wild explosion that gushed onto his tongue, hot and fast like a mento dropped in soda.

Her hips bucked with the powerful orgasm and she watched through blurry eyes as he drank the liquid that drenched her thighs and his face with long gulps and moans of appreciation. Using his tongue like a spoon, he scooped every last drop of fluid from her. The sloppy noises mixed with his bestial growls made it sound like a ravenous predator was devouring their prey between her legs.

"Rathym, *please*."

Deep crimson blotted out her vision as he unfurled his wings until all she saw was him, his scales shimmering with all the hues of red imaginable. They slowly beat behind him, keeping him afloat as he lined himself up with her entrance. She'd hardly recovered from her orgasm when he pressed his bottom cock against her soaking wet folds, easing himself inside.

Her body stretched to accommodate him, but it was a tight and difficult fit. Some part of her brain was cognitive enough to marvel that this was his *smallest* cock. She blinked back tears and attempted to swallow him up by rocking forward, but he placed a firm, claw-tipped hand on her stomach, strong enough to keep her still.

"Please. I need you to fill me."

"You are not ready yet," he said, his timbre deep and husky. "Patience. I will give you these cocks when your body can take them."

Dana wondered if it was desire that deepened his tone or the smoke that occasionally leaked from his snout. Glimpses into his mouth sometimes revealed traces of fire, like the first sparks from a flint stone.

"Distract me. It will go easier if my body is focused on…something else."

"Are you asking me to burn you?" His words almost sounded admonishing, but the gale of smoky breath that rippled out of his nostrils betrayed him.

"Yes."

"My treasure, you have too much pluck for your own good."

His head dipped to her neck. She tensed expectantly, but his kiss was tender, doting. She softened under his sweet kiss, her muscles relaxing.

Sharp teeth sank into her skin. She hissed as pain lanced through her, all of her attention drawn away from his cock to zero in on the spot where blood trickled down her neck. Rathym licked it away, pressing his tongue flat against the small wound. Her hands dug into the scales on his back so hard she would certainly have little scale-shaped imprints on her palms.

Abnormally hot breath teased her flesh, smoke pooling in between her clavicles. He leaned back and took her hand, kissing her palm before opening his mouth. A meager flame poured into her hand, hot but not too hot to bear.

He blew, sending the candle-sized flame up her arm. Hundreds of little fires blazed along her arm, across her chest, down to her belly button. This must be what a forest felt like when it burned. She was at the mercy of the flames and their master. It was so hot, but all she could do was writhe through the pain.

She didn't want them to be extinguished.

"Hotter," she breathed.

Rathym's wings shivered behind him. Without removing the barest tip of his cock, he flew them to another surface and settled above her, lifting her left leg over his shoulder. He licked the bone of her ankle, his tongue as hot as the flames on her skin as he laved the arch of her foot. With a soft breath, another little fire appeared on her big toe, then traveled up her leg like leaves in a breeze.

Ever so slowly, he pushed himself farther inside. Her pain sensors were torn between the flames and the unnatural stretching of her body, struggling to accept every inch of his cock.

"Oh my god," she breathed, nearly blind from the overwhelming pain and pleasure. The room went out of focus. As though he sensed her over-stimulation, his fires extinguished but for the barest trace of smoke softly whipping along her arms. "Oh, god, Rathym."

"Be still. Your body has never had to accommodate the size of me. I do not want to break you, my treasure."

With spotted vision, Dana wondered how he was he staying so still when their locked bodies craved friction.

Rathym took her hand and wrapped her fingers around the length of his top cock. She pressed his ribbed length against her belly as she stroked him, watching the pearl at the tip of his weeping cock grow with every stroke. She ran her thumb over the bead and used it as lubricant for his shaft, eliciting a tortured growl as he pushed further inside her. Translucent liquid continuously leaked onto her until he was sliding between her stomach and her hand with ease.

The sensation of his bestial growl that rumbled through her whole body paired with all the other stimulus took away any words she may have had to exclaim her pleasure, and he simultaneously drove himself even farther. Her walls stretched and contracted around him, stiffening in a muscle-jerking spasm, while an orgasm fought to wrest control of every fiber of her being. Her

86

inner walls clenched around his cock and she saw him watching her as he stuffed her poor cunt with even more of his impossible length.

Finally, he was buried as far as he could go, leaving at least a hand's length between his heavy sack and the spot her pussy clung to him. She could visibly see the spot where he filled her insides, all the way to her organs, her belly bulging with the gift of his cock stuffing her completely, utterly full. She couldn't imagine how it would feel, how much larger the swell would be, if it were his larger cock.

She couldn't help but think how much better her stomach looked bulging with his cock as opposed to being rounded with Jackson's baby. The mere sight of her surprisingly pliant body accepting almost all of him nearly crashed her over the next wave, and when she flicked her gaze up to see him mesmerized by the sight as well, she felt her clit pulse.

"You take my cock so well, little treasure." His tone was reverent and steady. He caressed her bloated belly and shivered as though the feeling teased his cock from the outside in. "Now come around my cock like a good girl."

She *was* a good girl. He trailed a finger down the swell of her belly to the pulsing nub right above where her body cinched around his cock. He barely ran his finger over it before she came undone, her cunt squeezing his massive length.

"Very good. You're doing so well."

She hardly heard him over her cries of intense

pleasure, but she felt him rocking his hips, driving himself through the tunnel he'd paved within her. His body tensed and he grunted. Suddenly, she felt a strong torrent of come cascade into her, his heavy, warm stream spouting into her so powerfully it wracked more pleasure from her limp, used body.

When the flow ceased, he pulled out of her with a wet *pop* and let the still half-hard cock fall between them. Dana whimpered as her pussy fluttered around the hot liquid steadily pouring from her to puddle around them.

"Hush, my treasure. Don't worry. I won't waste this seed, when your starving cunt obviously craves it so. It's rightfully yours. My little treasure's cunt wishes to be bred, to be filled and swelled with my seed."

She leaned onto her elbows to watch as he used his ribbed cock to play in their combined fluids. The creamy white substance of his and the slick clear moisture of hers mixed together, the spot where they converged sopping wet, a trail of white webbed between her thighs and his balls. He placed his top cock under the trickling stream until the fancy flared tip was covered like a glazed treat, then shoved it back inside.

It was difficult to tear her eyes away, but she glanced up to see him just as enthralled with the tantalizing sight. She watched as he shoveled that sticky, hot mess right back inside of her.

"You are magnificent," he said as he retreated from her to scoop up more of the slimy fluids and jam them back inside, some dripping out and following the curve of her ass. He repeated this motion, letting the full bulb of his cock pop in and out, an unbearable tease, as he marveled at her. "I cannot believe you are able to take me. I will fill your cunt with my come until you burst, and then I will plug you up and listen to you slosh with my seed."

It was too much. The sight of him literally *playing* with their mess crested her over another wave. She stared him in the eye as she reached down, wet her fingers in their combined come, then rubbed her clit in wild circles as he forced more of the warm substance back inside. She felt something stroke her cheek and turned toward it gratefully, opening her mouth for his tail.

She used her other hand to steady herself while his tail fucked into the back of her throat, just the way she liked it. The bumps on his tail rubbed against her tongue. Her hips rocked, the slimy mess slipping wetly beneath her movement. She could feel his bottom cock re-hardening, the stiffness of it pressing against the seam of her ass, the pressure of it alone making her ride the tip of his top cock harder.

He took her cue and drove all the way into her with a grunt. The full, fist-sized head of his cock *popped* into her despite her body's resistance. Their moans became a symphony with the sound of their mess squelching between their absolutely drenched thighs. He plunged into her again and again, the ribs of his inhuman cock massaging her insides. He pushed whatever come was still inside her back to the top as his thrusts became erratic.

"You are so beautiful. I'm going to fill you up. Can

you handle another load, little treasure?"

"Y-yes. Fill me," was all she could manage as she lost her ability to suck, then her ability to move at all. She fell back, one hand on her stomach to feel him moving inside her.

All of her motor functions shut off. There was nothing left of her except the gut-wrenching orgasm. She distantly and yet acutely felt the second round of his seed gush into her, the unyielding stream prolonging her toe-curling orgasm.

As feeling returned to her body, she felt the spot where their bodies were joined, where there was no fissure for his seed to escape. It amazed her that there was still so much length left outside of her. Curious, she reached down and gripped the extra length of him that couldn't fit. About four inches of his cock remained below where her body held on to him so tightly, his come filling her to the brim. She looked down at the roundness of her belly. It should be unimaginable that she could be so full, but here she was, filled with not only his unfeasible length but also brimming with his liquid.

Rathym's arms flexed around her. An animalistic growl vibrated their connection as he pressed his tongue to the spot he'd bit.

"You did so well," he breathed. "I'm so proud of you."

Pride bloomed from her core, filling every inch of her. The emotion she found in all three of his beautiful irises would've been enough to bring tears welling in her own, but at that same moment he eased out of her. They both gasped at the sensation of the bucketfuls of come spurting out of her in a rush of sloppy heat to join the messy pool around them and drip off the table. She felt his stiff bottom cock, hard and ready for the next round, twitch under her ass.

Rathym growled. Seemingly unable to help himself, he tilted upward and sank his freshly stiffened bottom cock back into her abused hole, trapping the rest of the warm liquid inside. She moaned, her flesh still sensitive, but he didn't move. He simply plugged her up.

Rathym's rested on her chest. The rubber-like spikes that crowned his head gently swayed under her fingers. His arms remained around her until he caught his breath and scooped her up.

He flew them out of the tunnel to their little waterfall oasis. The smooth rocks were cool under her feet. His breath of fire brought the water to a nice, comfortable steam.

Rathym bathed her with herbal soap. Feather-soft, doting touches caressed her skin, which somehow had only a twinge of pink where the fire should have burned her flesh. Special attention was given to the redness of her ass cheek where he'd slapped her pretty good— though to be fair, she did deserved it—and extra time went to washing her thighs.

"You take such good care of me."

Rathym met her gaze with eyes full of adoration. "You are my treasure. I'll always take care of you."

"I'm glad I'm your treasure."

She meant it. The words rolled off her tongue like

breathing. They filled her lungs and revitalized her. Nothing had felt so true in her life, other than perhaps the call to her passion, writing, but passions could be neglected if not practiced and nurtured. This thing she felt for Rathym couldn't be ignored.

She took the soap and began the same slow, affectionate ministrations he'd given her, tracing his scales and watching how the suds raced down his broad back. She ran the soap down with the grain of his sharp scales and chased it with her other hand. With every stroke against his glistening plates, she admired the wealth of hues held within every single scale. He was so beautiful, so breathtaking that it was impossible to put into words.

When they returned home, neither bothered to put on the fancy elven clothing. After rubbing her down with an ointment for the barely-there burns, they remained glued to each other as if magnetized. Dana typed while Rathym sat nearby, trailing his claws up and down her arm and reading over her shoulder. The only time he stepped away was to make dinner, and even then Dana couldn't help but take a break to snuggle his waist.

By the time she followed him to the nest, the only reason they hadn't come together again was his insistent worry that her body required rest before accepting him again.

"But you've already injected me with part of the healing salve. Shouldn't that mean I can have another dose?"

Rathym squinted at her until realization tugged his

mouths. He was in his full form, his two heads bent low to encircle her. A forked tongue slid through his lips as the other head responded.

"It does not work like that, my greedy treasure."

"But we could pretend it does. I think I need more—you know, to ease the pain." She wriggled in his grasp, but he held fast, trapping her like a snake with its prey.

"Are you truly in pain?"

She giggled. Of course he wouldn't understand her sarcasm.

"Speaking of magic elixirs, should we…" She bit her tongue. Something he'd said in the throes of passion had been nagging in the back of her mind. As hot as it'd been to hear him talk about *filling her with his seed*, she didn't want to *actually* be bred. Last time someone had wanted to impregnate her, it'd ended with an attempt on her life. "I mean, do I need to worry about having little dragon babies? Or…eggs?"

"No. We cannot conceive."

Relief swept through her. A long, coarse tongue licked her face, then he nuzzled both of her cheeks in a Dana sandwich.

"But that does not stop my body's natural desire to breed you, to fill you up and trap my seed inside, to see your belly full and swelled. As is the way. Now go to sleep."

The emotions that welled inside her heart were foreign, far from the emotion she'd named *love* with Jackson. Whatever this was, it was new. New and different and equally as terrifying as it was thrilling. She craved more of it.

Lying between his heads, completely and utterly surrounded by him, she could almost forget that she had a life and family outside of this cave.

Chapter 12
Rathym

Rathym's dreams were filled with his mate. The subtle dip of her waist, the feminine swell of her hips. Drops of water beading on her alluring bronze skin. In his dreams, he bathed himself in her light, the warmth of her setting ablaze a roaring fire to rival the Great Flame.

When he woke, the warmth was gone, replaced by a hollow ache.

His claw was bare, other than a Dana-sized imprint on the blanket. Frantic, he checked the faint thrum of their strengthening mate bond, which was even louder now that they'd coupled. There was no sign of danger. No sign of fear. Which could only mean one thing.

She left.

Fear niggled at the back of his mind, but he stamped it down with anger.

Rage.

An all-consuming fury filled Rathym. It seeped into all the pores he'd allowed filled by hope. Hope for what? For love?

Love was a thieving, misguided thing. A fickle emotion that drove the heart to blind the mind. Those under love's spell destroyed their own lives in ignorant bliss. To have been tricked so thoroughly in his old age was laughable. It was not the first time he was carried away by such a cliché, but last time he'd been only a boy of ninety years, not even a full-grown male. Anyone else he'd loved in any capacity had perished.

He checked the dining table. No note was scrolled for him on the blank sheets of parchment. The quill and ink he'd gifted her appeared untouched since last night. How would he endure the reckoning of Luvon's murderer whilst worried about his lost treasure? What if something happened before he could retrieve her? He had no idea how to keep her safe in the human world. His fearful wrath raised his fisted claw, ready to strike a blow to her beloved typewriter, when a rustle at the cave's entrance steadied him. He downshifted so he could meet her face to face when he demanded an explanation.

"Oh, good, you're awake!"

Dana reached for him. His muscles tensed in response, not wanting to shed the threads of fear weaved into his sinew. It was difficult not to allow his body to pop out of his smaller form with the height of his emotion. She didn't seem to notice. How was she able to trust so easily? He'd been close to destroying his own property because—because why?

"Where were you?" he demanded. Hard as he tried, he could not keep the serrated edge from his tone.

"I hiked up to the tourist shop for some snacks, and you'll never guess what I saw."

She was out of breath, her words unsteady, her hands shaking.

"You dislike my food so?"

"What? No! You're a master chef. I just got a crazy craving for some hot cheesy puffs." She paused, seeming to assess him. "I didn't mean to scare you."

That she would pause her own distress to tend to his filled him with guilt.

He forced his shoulders to relax and pressed his lips to her forehead. She would never know just how close he'd been to a huge mistake that would have cost him everything. *Everything*, because nothing in his hoard mattered compared to his human treasure.

A crumpled piece of parchment was scrunched in her hand. The source of her worry. A perfect depiction of her face was plastered above red lettering. She held it out for him to inspect further.

"They think I'm missing. I haven't spoken to my mom or my sister and who knows what story Jackson is telling everyone. Certainly not the truth!"

She paced the long side of the table, gesturing wildly as she spoke. Her bottom lip slipped behind worried teeth. She ran to her luggage and dug, coming up with the small device she'd planned to contact her employer with on their first morning together.

"Rathym, I *have* to call my mom. I really should go show everyone that I'm okay."

She spoke hesitantly, carefully studying his face. He hated that. Hated that she felt the need to tread so carefully for him. Hated that he'd put her in such a position. Hated that he was not strong enough to let her go, even as he knew he was not strong enough to make her stay, either.

If only she knew what he'd been willing to do moments ago. He would have destroyed the beautiful words she'd written in the process. Would have ruined the image of him in her mind. Now here she was, pleading with him to believe in her. To trust that she would return to his side.

His hesitance cast a dejected shadow over her beautiful features. She stepped closer, cradling his face in her soft hands.

"I will come back to you. But I have to let my family know I'm okay." She kissed the side of his mouth. "I know where I belong."

"Say it."

"I belong here. I belong here, with you."

He nodded curtly. The ache in his chest restricted his breathing.

"You must go, then." He had to rip the unwilling words from his throat, and still they sounded brittle, like they would fall apart in his claws. "They're worried about you."

He leaned down until their foreheads met, his arms encircling her trim waist. He held her for many beats of his hearts, her little hands pressed against his chest, her ambrosial and honey scent permeating his senses. When she pulled away, his arms released her with great reluctance.

"You have one day," he told her. She was lucky he had a reckoning to attend.

"Two."

A low growl escaped his throat, but his fearless mate stared him down until he nodded.

"Thank you." Her gaze drifted over his shoulder. "What's that?"

He turned. A shimmering gold envelope spun lazy circles over the dining table. The elegant swirls of magic weren't the popping fireworks of the council. It wasn't an urgent message.

"Great Flame take me," he grumbled. It was probably Ryuu and Anabraxus inviting him to dinner, or something equally trivial. "Two centuries. Why must I be bothered now?"

The envelope unraveled when he came near. It unfurled like a long tongue until it was a scroll, scribed with glittery black letters whirling across the page.

Sir Rathym Odrydimere,
You are cordially invited to celebrate the late King Luvon with us at the New Illuminated Ballroom on the next full moon. In honor of the fair King Luvon and

the young Princess Riniya, we will drink and dance knowing their sparks remain in our hearts.

We hope to see you and your plus-one on the dance floor.

Interesting. The remaining elves had erected a new grand ballroom in the fire kingdom? The use of the Fireborn term for soul was another curiosity. Whatever group arranged this party and sent the invitations must be a mix of species. He'd seen plenty of interspecies mingling on his errand to the council headquarters, but for some reason, he was still a tad surprised.

"A party?" Dana exclaimed. "A party with *elves*! Can we go?"

Rathym grimaced. Part of him wished he'd sent her off before opening the letter, while another rejoiced that she would want to go anywhere with him. He rolled the scroll up tightly and shoved down the knots forming in his stomach.

"It will be full of stuffy immortals and semi-mortals, and a handful of grieving elves. But if you wish to go, we will."

"What's wrong?"

"Nothing."

"You can talk to me, you know." As always, his treasure saw right through him. She smoothed away at the scales on his forearm. When he avoided her gaze, she leaned into his vision, searching his features. At once, her face lit brighter than the Great Flame. "Is this about your princess friend?"

"Yes." The scroll crumpled in his hand. He wanted to vomit the thoughts from his roiling stomach, the words that had festered inside him for two centuries. But how could he? Where would he start? So, he started with the truth. "I failed her. I failed them both."

He saw his own heartbreak mirrored in Dana's eyes. She said nothing, just continued her comforting touch. In that compassionate silence, she created space for him to purge. To grieve.

"I was not a good choice for regent. Everyone knew that. But Luvon was an optimist. He never thought it would truly come to it. Said he would want his most trusted friend to help guide Riniya. The fool said it in front of a high priest!" His fist decimated the scroll. "I'd gone to take care of personal business in my homeland. I was still juggling my responsibilities as Grand Commander. When the attack came, she was defenseless. I should have been there."

"Oh, Rathym. I'm so sorry."

"Two hundred and sixteen years later, they've finally caught the dragon responsible for stealing Luvon from his daughter. From his kingdom." He nearly choked on the lump in his throat. The scroll went up in flames. "From me. If Luvon were alive, the elves never would have fallen. This *thief* has lived for two centuries without consequence. Now he will get his reckoning."

"Is that like a trial?"

"Of a sort." He chucked the burnt letter into the

cooking pit. It was his turn to pace the long table "Tonight, he will receive the punishment befitting of his crime. Two hundred years too late."

"Maybe it will feel better to know that it's over." Her tone was light. Optimistic.

"It has been over for a long time." His hands balled into fists. His voice ground out through clenched teeth. "There's no such thing as closure when you live without your loved ones for three times a mortal's lifespan."

Dana was silent. He couldn't bring himself to face her. Her cheery outlook was adorable, but it wasn't *real*. Acting like everything would work out was impractical. He'd spent too long steeped in the truth of his grief to hang it up now.

Feather-soft fingers trailed up his back. He shivered at her touch, his muscles contracting further. She wrapped her arms around his waist, her palms splayed on either side of his hips. He resisted at first, too stubborn to give in, but she exhaled over his scales and the warmth of her breath forced him to soften.

"I'm sorry you went through that. It must have been incredibly difficult to live without your friends for so long. Thank you for confiding in me." She kissed his scales, an apology in every brush of her lips. "I'm sorry I won't be there with you."

If she knew what the reckoning entailed, she would not wish to accompany him. He shifted until her damp cheek was flush against his chest, his claws plunging into her hair.

"It's all right, my treasure. I have acquaintances there. I won't be alone." He kissed the top of her head, inhaling a deep breath of her scent. He would miss her greatly. Especially after the ceremony, when he would return to an empty nest. "You must prove your safety to your family. That's what's important right now."

Her arms tightened around his waist. Her soft lips pressed against the smooth surface of his chest. The light touch made his hearts flood his groin with heat.

A delicate moan slipped Dana's lips. He dipped his head to swallow it and pushed his way into her mouth to surround her tongue with his. She opened for him eagerly.

When the scent of her arousal reached his nostrils, there was nothing in the world that could keep him from watching her unravel. From filling her with enough seed that she would spend her life swelled with child if she were a dragon. He raised her dress and planted his knee between her thighs, driving her backward until she lay on the table, her legs dangling.

If she'd planned to protest, he didn't allow it. He hiked her legs over his shoulders and kneeled before her. Her sensitive pink flesh glistened like a dew-coated lily, her sweet scent engulfing him like a fresh bouquet. He slipped his tongue through her petals, flicking her clit just to watch her writhe.

"So beautiful," he murmured before delving his tongue through her again, pulling back to watch her muscles clench, her perfect body fluttering around

103

nothingness, searching for him. Longing for him. Waiting to overflow with his seed. "What a beautiful sight your little cunt is, my treasure."

Her melodious sounds rose in octaves as he again tasted her and pulled away to watch her cunt desperately seeking him. A fresh coating of slickness leaked out of her. He murmured his appreciation and bowed his chin to nuzzle his face in the sweet nectar, coating himself from snout to chin.

"Rathym, please."

"Please what, my treasure? Use your words."

"Please make me come," she moaned. A dainty hand appeared before him. She sought to rub herself free of the ache, but he took her wrist and held it against her hip.

"I'll take care of you," he said with a cluck of his tongue. "Haven't I always taken good care of my treasure?"

"Y-yes."

Before the word was out, he plunged a finger inside her. Her hips jerked, sending a flirtatious wave of her scent through his senses. He suctioned his mouth around her clit and sucked, flicking the tight bud with his tongue. Her hips bucked against him as he added another finger. Her hands flew to his horns in a death-grip as her inner walls constricted around him and another rivulet of liquid heat leaked around his fingers.

"Rathym," she pleaded.

"Yes, my treasure?"

"I want—I want you to touch yourself, too."

He groaned against her cunt, which made her drive herself over his face again. He removed his loincloth and gripped himself, the top, most swollen of his cocks. He stood above her and stared down at her bare body, stroking himself for her to see.

"What else?" A coil of smoke escaped his mouth.

"I want to be covered in your come." Her voice was steady now, although her eyelids fluttered.

He growled. He would much rather pump her full of his seed, to send it deep inside her womb. But there was no reason he couldn't do both, although his body's mating instincts wanted to revolt. He returned to his knees and plunged three fingers inside her, sucking rhythmically on her clit. Her soft moans and her scent made his cock pulse in his hand, but he did not slow and added another. He could feel his balls filling with seed, his bottom cock leaking just as much as the one in his grip, begging to be buried deep inside his treasure's willing holes.

Dana's body wracked against him. He could tell she was close, so he withdrew and rose to meet her desperate gaze. Without slowing the strokes on his top cock, he sank his bottom one into her in one swift motion.

The surprised bliss that graced her features made his cocks weep.

"Watch," he commanded. Her eyes shot open just as his seed splashed in long ropes over her stomach, her chest, her open mouth.

His greedy treasure moaned. Her back arched as her

tight cunt clutched his bottom cock, which was ready to explode, but he held back until the last drop of his seed painted her. Her fingers trembled as she ran them through his come and brought them, dripping, to her mouth, then back through his seed until she reached her clit. Her orgasm visibly ripped through her the moment her come-covered fingers circled her taut bud.

The sight was too much. Rathym rammed into her with a lurch, lifting her hips to reach as far inside her as he could possibly reach.

He painted her insides the same creamy white as her stomach.

When his stream finally subsided and her body stopped twitching, she giggled. He couldn't help but smile with her, until they were both laughing like fools.

The moment couldn't last forever, though. They both had places to be. A quick stop at the spring, and then they returned home to say their goodbyes. Not their final goodbyes, although it might as well have been as far as Rathym's hearts were concerned. They felt helpless, each beat of their rhythm out of tune as he watched her redress, lacing up her hiking boots.

"Oh! I almost forgot." She pulled something from her pocket. "I saw this and it made me think of you."

The little trinket was made of imitation metal that was colored to look like gold. In the center of the faux-gold was a teardrop-shaped faux ruby. More guilt rose with the tide of emotions within him. While he'd been blind with anger and fear, she had been thinking of him.

106

"It's beautiful. I shall treasure it always." He motioned her to wait as he gathered a bag of gold coins from their designated pile. "Take these. Get as many snacks and trinkets as you like."

She giggled, the sound more beautiful than any enchanted wind chime. "I'm not sure of anywhere I can use these, but thank you, Rathym. It means a lot."

"I haven't told you, but there is another reason I am enamored with you." He took her hand in his and kissed each of her knuckles. "Why I fantasize about filling you, rounding you. Why it is difficult to see a single drop of seed be wasted." He kissed her forehead, then leaned close to her ear. "My body recognized you as its mate the moment you fell into my lair. Naturally, that makes me want to take you over and over, to fill you with my seed and trap it inside, whether we're capable of conceiving or not."

He watched her cheeks warm and heard her heart speed up, the sweet scent of her desire reaching his nostrils.

"Come back to me, treasure. We belong together."

"I know. I will."

He watched her pack her things, barely restraining himself from wrapping her in his arms and forcing her to stay. *Stay with me*, he wanted to beg. *Stay.*

She cast a small smile over her shoulder as she ascended the tunnel. His hearts broke with her departure, thudding mournfully in his chest like an elven funeral dirge. What if he never saw her again? There were so many unknowns in the world. Too many. She could be swept away in an untamed fire or brutally attacked in her sleep. Damn her mortal disposition, her human flesh and brittle bones.

He would have to trust her, just as she'd requested. So he shoved that worry away and replaced it with another. Ivaan Kovgroff would face his reckoning this evening, and Rathym would not miss it for the world.

Chapter 13
Dana

Just like last time, the normal folks innocently browsing the little shop's goods and baubles ogled Dana's strange dress. She pretended not to notice because, honestly, hadn't anyone been to the renaissance fair before? If only people would dress however the hell they wanted *all* the time, then it wouldn't be so out of place for a woman to wear the royal garb of an elven princess to the gas station.

"Do you have a phone charger I could borrow?" she asked the teenager behind the counter.

"I think you have to buy one," he replied casually, not even glancing at her from over his cell phone.

"Please, it's the same type of phone in your hand.

Can you just let me plug it in for a few minutes?" When her desperate tone didn't catch his attention, she waved the missing poster in front of the plexiglass. "Look, this is me! I have to call my mom and tell her I'm okay. Please!"

That did the trick. He held up an index finger and disappeared into the back, returning with a slight jog to his step.

"Thank you," she said as she accepted the black cord and block from under the plastic window.

"You can take it to the bathroom for some privacy. Here's the key."

"Thank you."

The bathroom was surprisingly well-kept for such a rural attraction site, and the stall was blessedly empty. Her phone took a few minutes to hold a charge. As her anxiety built, she tapped her finger on her knee and bounced on the balls of her feet.

Her phone vibrated for five straight minutes with missed calls, texts, messages, and notifications, almost all of them from her mom and sister, rendering the phone useless until the buzzing stopped.

"Oh, god."

They really must think she was dead. She'd been so swept up in her surreal reality ever since Rathym plucked her from the last working toilet stall she'd seen before this one. It had been easy to lose herself, to let her life be rerouted, supplanted from her boring existence. Especially after nearly becoming a tragic late-night news episode. How long had she been in that cave, living a fantastical daydream?

She should have pressed Rathym to let her call them sooner. Then again, he might've denied her until they grew closer. Even now, she knew it was still difficult for him to agree. She hadn't missed the signs of fear and anger when he'd woken up to an empty nest.

Her mom's phone only trilled for half a ring before she picked up, her voice shaky. "Dana! Dana?"

"Mom!"

"Dana! Samantha, it's Dana!" her mom yelled into the phone. Dana held the phone away from her ear until her volume went back down, her tone quivering with barely contained tears. "*Bayiku*, what is this?"

"It's a long story. What has Jackson been saying?"

Her sister's voice called something too far for the phone to catch, growing louder as the phone was rustled and placed on speaker.

"That *bajingan* says you dumped him on a hiking trip and then never came home," Samantha said with her typical attitude. "But that's impossible. You wouldn't dump him—and if you were going to, I would've known well before he did!"

Dana laughed. It was true. Even in the early days of her and Jackson's relationship, Samantha nagged her to leave him. She would deflect, citing reasons like *oh but he pays the bills while I write*, or *oh but he supports my dream*, and *oh but I owe him so much for all he's done for me*. She'd been willfully blind to the fact that he was

111

steadily taking said dream away from her and cocooning her in false freedom, a cage the shape of a family home.

"Yeah. No, he—uh—" she stuttered. She should've considered how much she wanted to tell them. She couldn't exactly say where she'd been. She would tell Sam. Sam would believe her, probably even be envious. Her sister was the one who got her hooked on steamy fantasy romance novels that sounded eerily similar to her new life.

Her mom, however, was a different story. She came from a different world, a different time. Even though her mom was educated, she still struggled with some modern-day behaviors, like most parents do. For instance, even though she'd never said it out loud, Dana knew her mom strongly disapproved of her decision to move in with a man she wasn't married to.

"He pushed me off a cliff."

Her mom gasped. Samantha went quiet.

"Are you all right?" Sam asked a moment later. Their mother's sobs grew distant. Her sister's hushed voice got closer. "You're off speaker for a sec."

"I'm fine. I'll tell you everything when I see you, okay? Just don't let Mom go off the deep end."

"Okay. Glad you're safe."

After a few more minutes of reassurances, Dana promised to get a car home and hung up.

The driver of the old Ford Taurus that picked her up tried his best to make small talk but dropped it when she basically iced him out. She didn't care to talk to anyone, let alone a stranger in the front seat. The conversation she was bound to have with her mom and the cops was daunting. It had to be done, yes—but it would be the most uncomfortable thing she'd ever endured, and she wasn't excited to tell a bunch of lies.

Her whole life, she'd been the peacekeeper. Between her mom and sister arguing over Sam's grades. Between her mom and grandmother over her mom's decision not to move back home. Between her sister and their cousins, who teased Sam's voice every time they visited because she spoke more like their father.

Dana had spent a long time people-pleasing and hardly ever considered setting boundaries. She'd nearly given in to Jackson's relentless badgering about having kids simply to keep the peace. Hell, she'd spent the past week in a dragon's lair partially because she didn't want to hurt his feelings.

Although she didn't regret that last one.

Rathym. Her heart constricted at the thought of him. She hoped he would be okay while she was gone. His separation anxiety was concerning. At first, she'd wondered if it was a trait common among his species. Now, she knew it was born from the tragic loss of his friends. How painful it must be to harbor that grief and blame for two whole centuries. It definitely explained a lot.

The car squeaked to a stop. She thanked the driver, stepped outside, and was immediately clobbered by her family.

"Oh, *bayiku*. I was so worried!" wailed her mother.

"I'm sorry, Mom, I should've called sooner."

"Could you have?" Sam asked. "Were you surviving in the woods?"

The image of herself using sticks to make a fire or sharpening them into spears for hunting made her snort. Another image came to mind, of a tall, broad, scaled hunk poring over an old cook fire, preparing hearty, scrumptious meals, cocks swaying with his steps. Even with the hours-long drive home, she hadn't come up with a believable story for her mother. Or the police, for that matter.

"Well, actually, I met a man who…lives off the land. He helped me recover from the fall."

Over her mom's shoulder, Sam slapped a hand over her mouth. She asked a silent question with her arched brows and jutted neck, to which Dana responded with a sly smile. Their mother abruptly stopped the embrace to assess Dana at arm's length.

"A man? Recover? Are you hurt? Oh, *atiku*!"

"Mom, relax. Please. Let's go inside—"

"*Ora*. We go straight to the police!" She abruptly stepped away from Dana and extended her hand with the keys already poised. "You stayed with a man in the woods after being pushed by your fiancé—"

"*Fiancé?*"

Samantha eyed her over the top of their mom's blue sedan. "Oh, yeah. That's the other part of what Jackson's been saying. You dumped him after he proposed to you

114

at the top of a mountain. I guess he thought if it sounded like he loved you enough to marry you, it would be less suspicious." She snorted. "It definitely made me suspicious! I told you he was lying, Mom."

"*Ya wis*, you did."

"At least let me run in and get my old pair of glasses and take out these dry contacts," Dana grumbled.

The spare lenses were adequate, and at least they were more comfortable. Her eyes couldn't take another squirt of eye drops. She slumped into the seat behind her mom. She'd expected to have to talk to the police, but she wasn't looking forward to it. Her palms were clammy and her mouth suddenly felt deprived of saliva. Between her discomfort and Samantha's deadpan stare, it was difficult to pay attention to her mom's relentless questions. Samantha's entire body was angled toward her, watching every twitch of her face, undoubtedly trying to gauge what pieces of her answers were truthful.

The police station in Witmore—which doubled as a community center—was set up for some kind of meeting. Dana walked around rows of rusty folding chairs, through a hallway with multiple flickering lights, and knocked on a door cracked open by a brick on the floor.

"Hang on!"

After a few moments of scuffling, a police officer whipped open the door. His peppered mustache featured yellow mustard tips that matched his red-and-yellow-spotted fingers. His cheeks smacked around a mouthful of what she assumed was hoagie by the flashes of lunch meat and white bread in his open mouth.

"Come on in, ma'am." He held the door open with his hand way up at the top, craning so that she could duck under his arm awkwardly. "What can I do for ya?"

"I-I'm here to report a crime?" She winced at how pathetic she sounded. She cleared her throat and tried again. "My boyfriend pushed me off a cliff in the Rockies."

She detailed her experience as truthfully as she could. The officer took her statement in stride, his thoughts indiscernible as he scribbled along to her voice. When she summed it all up, he nodded and clicked his pen a few times.

"Welp, I'll get this to the chief. Come back in the morning with all your belongings from the trip for evidence. This'n will probably go to the court, so I'd start lookin' for an attorney if I were you."

"A trial? But—"

"Sensitive case like this, we might'n be able to expedite it in front of Judge Larson."

"I don't have time for that. I have to—" She stopped in her tracks. She couldn't exactly say *I have to get back to my anxious dragon mate*. "I can't stay here."

The officer nodded, the motion void of any real empathy. He sniffed, his grubby mustache swishing. "All right, all right. We'll see what we can do, okay, ma'am? In the meantime, come on back in the morn'."

Dana helplessly agreed to his placating bullshit and

left. She found Samantha outside of the building, perched on top of a lopsided picnic table. Her mom was engaged in a conversation with a clearly unwilling officer at the end of the sidewalk. Their body language and proximity to the idling police car made it obvious that her mom had trapped the unsuspecting woman before she made it three steps from her vehicle. Judging by the officer's familiar behavior—lots of head shaking, palm raising, and a look of total bewilderment—she was struggling to understand her mom's rapid speech. Of course, none of that deterred her mom.

"Hey, should we get an escort to drop by Jackson's place with us so we can pick up your stuff?" Sam asked.

"Yeah, that's probably smart."

When they reached her old house, Jackson wasn't home. A small relief. With Sam's help, she gathered all necessary items and bagged them up in white trash bags, a total of two thirteen-quart bags containing all her things. Compared to Rathym's endless cave full of stuff, it seemed like an insignificant amount for one person. Did any of it really matter to her? Well, yeah, her laptop and books. But the bag full of clothes could remain or even be fodder for a fire as far as she cared. When she returned to Rathym, she didn't plan on wearing clothes. Unless she was simply in the mood to look like a fae princess.

For the hundredth time, she wondered if Rathym was holding up all right. She hated that he'd been going through all of that heavy stuff on his own. Wished that she could have relieved his burden even a little. Early on, she had wondered why he was so reclusive and grouchy, but she hadn't considered that he was going through something so traumatic.

Others might look at him like a monster in a cave, but she could no longer see him as anything but her *pisang goreng* lover, his crispy shell encasing a sweet, creamy center.

Chapter 14
Rathym

The enormous arena buzzed with activity. The general atmosphere teetered the line between hostile and somber. Rathym's anticipation grew at the sight of the roasting stage. Soon the sun would kiss the horizon, and the day he'd given up hope for would commence.

His claws tapped against his thigh as he searched for Anabraxus and Ryuu outside of the coliseum. Aside from his short visit to the council the other day, it had been a long time since he'd visited society, and even longer since he'd been in a crowd like this. He longed for his human's comforting touch along his scales, but he would settle for a familiar face.

The hushed whispers exchanged behind claws didn't help.

"It can't be."

"I swear, that's him!"

"The regent?"

"The Grand Commander!"

His frown felt like it was becoming permanent by the time he reached the edge of the arena. The outdoor coliseum was packed with bodies. Dragons in both shifts sat shoulder to shoulder and other creatures dappled the stands. Bodies bumped against him, people turning to glare at him before recognition hit.

Where the hell were Ryuu and Anabraxus?

"Excuse me, excuse me, sorry, pardon me." At the sound of Ryuu's voice, a flood of relief rushed out of Rathym in the form of a strangled sigh. "Kin! How good it is to see you. When Ana told me of your visit, I was thrilled! Well, not for the circumstances, but you know."

Rathym grumbled a greeting, his uneasy gaze darting around them. Luckily, his brother-in-arms recognized his stiffness for what it was. Ryuu guided him through the packed bodies until they had room to release their wings. They flew up the three flights of stands to the balcony and touched down in the box reserved for those who were close to the victim. The box consisted of Rathym, Anabraxus, Ryuu, and three elves. The sight of such a small group of people was like a stab to Rathym's gut. Elvendale had been full of people who loved Luvon, and yet there were so few left alive.

"Regent Odrydimere," one of the elves, Caundur, greeted him. The sound of his former title from an elf only twisted the knife lodged in his gut. "King Ludove would be grateful to see you here."

Rathym could do nothing but nod, his breath caught in lungs like amber. Somewhere between parting ways with his mate and this moment, he'd lost control of most of his functions. Caundur retreated, and Rathym returned his troubled gaze to the wide-open expanse of sand.

Ryuu gently nudged his shoulder. "How are you coping?"

"Quite all right, thank you." The words came out too harsh. He blew out a breath that sent smoke from his nostrils and shook his head, finally meeting his old friend's compassionate stare. "It—it's all a bit much."

"Aye."

"There he is, the big lump!" called a cheery female's voice from behind. "I knew you wouldn't miss this."

"Greetings, Anabraxus."

"*Greetings, Anabraxus.* That's what you sound like." She laughed and pressed a mug into his chest, which he gratefully accepted. "Figured you'd need this after, oh, forty centuries away from any living thing."

"Ana," warned Ryuu.

"I'm just saying. So, should I assume we won't see you at the ball?"

"You could, but you would be wrong. In fact, I have a plus-one." Pride welled in his hearts at the sight of his friends' surprised faces, a welcome feeling amongst the

121

grief-clouded air. He paused to sip his ale before adding, "My human companion. My mate."

Anabraxus slammed her hand over her mouth. "Not you, you're a Traditional Trelly! A *human*?"

"You'd better make a pit stop at Xerald's for some oil, old friend," Ryuu said with a chuckle. "I didn't think a human could handle a dragon without Xerald's mixture. It's magic, it is."

Anabraxus snorted and nodded emphatically. "A human. She doesn't mind all your junk? How big is your hoard these days, anyway?"

"I'll have you know—" Rathym began, but his sentence dropped like a boulder in the ocean as the commencement horn was blown.

The prisoner would soon be escorted into the arena. The box fell silent. All eyes turned to the sandy ground. Rathym took a few steps back and shifted, not trusting that he could maintain his downshift. From the spectacular view, Rathym could make out every knot and whorl of the burning table. The slabs of old wood would be engulfed in the flames of the reckoning.

The burnished door of the tunnel connecting the coliseum to the Iron Prison trembled. Rathym's hearts mimicked the thundering steps, his breath stuck inside his lungs, his fury hot smoke inside his mouth.

He wanted to be down there, to greet the murderer who was responsible for so much suffering with his own fire. He wanted to dole out the reckoning. But the rules were clear, and although he'd washed his hands of this society for many years, he wasn't prepared to stand upon the burning table for murder the same way this vile creature was about to.

The doors swung open.

The executioner stepped out first, a fierce, blood-red dragon with enormous curved horns and fire leaking from his eyes.

Rathym's throat grew exponentially hotter. He released the smoke building up inside him through his nostrils, attempting to quell the flame that wanted to erupt from his core.

Rage.

A heavy silver chain trailed behind the executioner. It clinked and chimed until he halted at the edge of the burning table, but the prisoner attached to it remained sheltered just inside the tunnel.

A Fireborn with the complexion of a carnation took the stand. Her downshifted form stood at the podium situated a few yards in front of the burning table, her voice ringing out clearly in the utter silence.

"Let today be remembered as a triumph," she started. "For today, we avenge our neighbor and ally, King Ludove. It is with heavy hearts and brightly burning sparks that we bestow the king's assailant his reckoning. Rejoice the Great Flame."

A murmur rippled through the crowd, but Rathym could not speak through the burning smoke that steadily poured through his clenched teeth. He'd allowed his full shift to complete, but his control over the flame within remained tenuous at best. The speaker was downplaying the centuries-long lack of information, lack of investigation, lack of care whatsoever for Ludove's case. How dare they call this kingdom an *ally*? The whole council had dropped the case the moment they thought no one was looking. That was no ally.

He wanted to skip this part and watch the flames whip the night sky. Patience was no longer within his capability. The sun was nestled on the precipice, the horizon nearly engulfed in twilight's rich navy hue, heralding the coming of the reckoning.

"Bring the prisoner forth."

The chains were pulled taut. He held his breath, ready to set eyes on the dragon that had ruined so many lives. For years, this was the sole purpose of Rathym's existence, this moment, this vengeful moment.

A frail figure emerged from the darkness. He was in his downshift, with a muzzle over his mouth and chains binding all of his limbs. He looked debilitated, malnourished, and old. Very old. The tips of his horns were sheared, but their stumps were the color of ash, as were his claws. He walked with his shoulders hunched, his gaze solely on his shuffling feet.

This was the assassin? This feeble thing?

"No." Fire poured from the edges of Rathym's mouth. "No."

Ryuu and Anabraxus tossed him worried looks. He didn't miss the concern that passed each between them when he downshifted to pace the box. Blackness encroached on the edges of his vision. He stopped at the railing and clung to the bar for stability as the coliseum seemed to sway under his feet.

The last sliver of sun disappeared.

The prisoner stepped onto the slab of wood.

"Ivaan Kovgroff," the announcer stated. "For the assassination of the Fair King Luvon, King of Elvendale, and for conspiracy to genocide, you face your reckoning today. State your last words."

Focus. Rathym's eyes strained against the pounding in his brain. The muscles in his biceps popped, his full form threatening to overtake him.

"I find myself full of regret. I accept my reckoning. May my damned spark spend eternity barred from the Great Flame."

No.

The final word was barely out of the prisoner's mouth before the executioner's flames reached the frail dragon. King Luvon's murderer cried out, his pained screams piercing the night sky with as much ferocity as the fire engulfing him.

But those pained screams did not bring Rathym joy. They did not ease his fury. The cleansing flames whipping against the velvet sky did not lessen the weight of the stones in his hearts. They were no balm to his charred spark.

"Rathym," Anabraxus spoke gently. "Are you all right?"

He shook his head. The world was out of focus, but

he noticed the same storm in Caundur's dilated pupils.

"What was the point of this?" Rathym growled.

"At least there was closure—"

"What good does that do?" he thundered. His shout turned all heads in the vicinity to him. "What good did any of this do!"

He took to the sky, pumping his wings with unnecessary force. He wanted to run to his beloved treasure, to lay his head in her lap, to feel her soft hands smooth his scales. He wanted to find her, bring her home, and never leave the comfort of her touch again. Never let her leave the safety of his cave again.

But she would not be in his cave. She was gone. She was somewhere she could get hurt, somewhere with dangers he didn't understand threatening her at every turn. He didn't want to return to his empty nest. He didn't trust himself to remain there instead of going to retrieve his treasure.

The grieving pool was the only other thing that would understand him in this state. He wept into the magma and shouted into the void until his voice was hoarse and his tears were only smoke.

His cave was achingly empty. The piles of precious junk didn't provide any comfort.

He created a shelf next to the bedding to hold the jars of magic oil he'd purchased after leaving the grieving pool. The jars taunted him with images of his beloved beneath him, on top of him, but he tried not to get swept away in visions of all the ways he wanted to ravish her. She wasn't here.

He took solace in the words on her pages. The characters were an obvious draw from their blossoming relationship, the bitter old dragon a painfully accurate depiction of himself. Some of the words made his hearts ache, knowing that his reluctance to let go of outdated traditions had hindered their connection. If only he'd released those old ways earlier. How much sooner would they have lain together? Just another false pretense he'd clung to for so many centuries. In the end, no tradition, no matter how steadfastly clung to, could fill a fractured heart. He'd learned that all too well in the past few hours.

After a while, he checked the sun's position. It felt as though no time had passed since she left. How would he ever get along without her to fill this empty space?

When had his cave become so utterly empty?

His neat piles were redundant. Suffocating. He was boarded up in a cage of his own making. Not even the enchanted wine bottle could put his worries at bay. There was a time, long ago, that he would have taken to the skies to ease his worries. When had he become so landlocked, so stuck in his ways? Why did a lone human female have to supplant his life in order for his eyes to open?

He struggled to keep from falling apart at the seams. Over the course of mere days, the blink of an eye to a dragon, his human treasure had *become* the thread that held his seams together. Stronger even than the most adept elven seamstresses. Without her, he would surely become a new pile to adorn the cold stone floor, one of crimson blood and gore.

An idea came to mind as he perused the books stacked neatly into separate genre-specific piles. There was still so much unused room in the lonely cave, and he had the time and power to create more if needed. Last time he'd rearranged, he'd caused a shift in the rocks that created new formations along the mountain. Cliff drops and hangs cropped up along the steep incline, rocks and boulders shifted. He would be more careful this time.

He decided to do something useful with this time separated from his mate. Something that would show her that he was a worthy partner. Something to prove he belonged to her just as much as she belonged to him.

Something that would keep his mind from reliving bright flames whipping against the night sky.

Chapter 15
Dana

Samantha knocked on the open door to Dana's childhood bedroom. She leaned against the frame and held up a plastic-covered silver tray.

"Yes, please!"

Sam kicked the door shut and plopped onto the bed beside her, extending a hand with two forks. Dana snatched one and removed the lid from the chocolate silk pie. Their favorite. Their mom's favorite, too. There was always one in their fridge growing up, especially after their dad left. Their mom bought the pies for herself, but the sisters would sneak into the kitchen past bedtime to share a late night treat. They always ate too much and yet childishly believed they'd been discreet. Sometimes they would use a knife and slowly shed little slivers of the pie, as though their mother wouldn't notice if they kept each bite small.

"So, what really happened out there?"

"You're going to be so jealous."

"Oh my god, just tell me!" Sam whined over a hefty bite. "I've been dying all day!"

Dana giggled and launched into her true story. Sam's expression traveled between shock, awe, and envy. Dana wrapped up the story with a shrug and a little *yep*. Her cheeks hurt from grinning at Sam's priceless reaction, eyebrows practically invisible in her hairline, the pie forgotten.

"So basically you're in love with a fucking *dragon* and if you don't get home to him *tomorrow* he's gonna come kill us all. *Asu edan*! Who are you, and what have you done with my sister?"

"Jesus, Sam. He would just come get me." Dana paused. "I think."

Knowing his anxiety and the difficult day he was enduring, it might be less pretty than she wanted to admit. Still, she had faith. She wanted to believe he would be understanding, given the full scope of her current situation. She plucked her glasses from her nose and rubbed them with the bottom of her shirt.

"I hope you're right because this shit with Jackson is just getting started. Nothing goes quickly through this small town's law system." Sam patted her knee. "But it's the right thing. That *bajingan* would just prey on another

130

woman, and she probably won't have a fierce new dragon boyfriend to *vanquish her foes*."

A sad truth. Dana scooped another chunk of chocolate mousse, her bright mood diminishing quickly.

"Hey, does your man have any friends?" Sam nudged her elbow and wiggled her brow.

Dana snorted. "If he does, I'll introduce you. But only if you don't tell that embarrassing story about my ninth birthday just to make people laugh."

"But it's a great icebreaker!"

"It's really not."

Dana chuckled. *Did* Rathym have friends? Turns out he was a high-ranking official, which wasn't surprising at all. He had the authoritative demeanor of someone used to giving orders. She tried to picture him at a social event, his brooding stare a warning to anyone considering approaching him. In her mind's eye, a former acquaintance offered him a drink. Perhaps he took it and downed it in one gulp, his sneer returning the moment it left his lips. In her daydream, the acquaintance morphed into a beautiful female dragon with four boobs and the perfect hourglass silhouette.

Now I'm just making shit up. Dana glowered at the next forkful of pie.

In the morning, Sam drove Dana back to the station, where she repeated her long-winded half-truth. The police chief listened thoughtfully, taking notes here and there, but mostly retaining eye contact. Behind him, his comrades picked apart her hiking pack with white plastic gloves.

Something felt off. What were they looking for? It all felt…wrong. Like she was a suspect and not a victim. The suspicion in the chief's eyes when he'd asked to photograph her injuries and she'd explained they weren't visible anymore had only ramped up the sense of *wrongness*. She kind of wished she'd lied about the whole thing. Or never brought it up to begin with.

"Here's the deal, Ms. Gretchens." The chair squeaked under the large man as he shifted forward. He rubbed a fat set of fingers over his gray-speckled beard and cleared his throat. "We can take this to trial. Or we can set up a meeting with Mr. Willsburn and try to work something out."

"What does that even mean?"

The portly older man tapped his pen against his notepad. "Mr. Willsburn approached us earlier. Some of these things don't add up to what Mr. Willsburn reported—"

"Of course they don't. If they did, that would mean he turned himself in!"

"All right, all right." He leaned back and raised his palms. "Suit yourself. I've already spoken to Judge Larson. Lucky for us, he has time this Friday. Let's just give mediation a shot. What could it hurt?"

Dana rose quickly enough that her chair clattered to the floor. "With all due respect, I am not interested in mediation. Jackson tried to *kill me*. I'll see the judge, but I'm bringing my attorney and pressing charges."

She gleaned a brief look at the chief's stunned face before it hardened into something much less friendly. He looked as though he expected her to incriminate herself with the next words out of her mouth.

She didn't give him any satisfaction, instead turning on her heel. She tripped over the fallen chair, cursing as she caught herself ass-up. She barely heard the chief state the time and place behind her. She'd lived in this little unincorporated town her whole life. She already knew where their one judge and makeshift courtroom were.

"What's wrong?" Samantha asked the moment she got in the car.

Before Dana could answer, angry tears still burning in her eyes, she noticed movement in the sky.

"Oh, no. Drive!"

Sam obeyed immediately, casting the sky a frightened glance. "Where am I going?"

"Go to the road we used to drive down to smoke in high school." The rural road led out into the country boondocks with houses miles away from their neighbors.

Samantha, always down for an adventure, stepped on the gas and delivered them to the sight of many fond and embarrassing memories. She parked on the side of the road, where Dana hopped out and paced to the tree

133

line for a little added privacy, pushing her glasses farther up her nose. Sam followed, clearly excited for the chance to meet a real-life dragon.

Rathym downshifted mid-flight, landing in front of her in his reptilian form. A peek at Sam showed she was already doing better at accepting the existence of a mythical creature than Dana had at first, although her hazel eyes were wide and alert.

"What are you doing here? We agreed I had until tonight."

"I felt your strong emotion. Are you all right?" His deep voice was unyielding, the ancient dragon in him shining through.

"You could've been seen. What will I do if you're shot down?"

Rathym's ridged brow slammed down. He scoffed.

"That would not happen." A puff of fire and smoke leaked from his jaw as he spoke. "Men and their weapons will not stop me from protecting what is mine."

Samantha's sharp inhale drew both of their attention.

"Who is this?"

"Rathym, this is my sister, Sam. Sam, Rathym."

"Pleased to meet you." Rathym dipped his head reverently, cupping Sam's hand and pressing it to his mouth.

Sam fanned herself with her free hand. She caught Dana's eye and mouthed, *so sexy!*

"I'm sorry I worried you, but you have to trust me."

Dana's cheeks burned, the familiar panic over upsetting someone threatening to stutter her heartbeat. "I need to spend some extra time here to deal with Jackson and those idiot cops."

Rathym's rough stoicism hardened into something much more terrifying. "That is not what we agreed."

"Rathym," she stated firmly. He stood rigid but allowed her touch on his smooth abdomen. "I want to come home. But I have to do this first. I have to make sure he can't hurt someone else."

His silence was heavy, but she laid her head on his chest and wove her arms around his waist. His scales pricked her fingers as she ran them up and down, nuzzling into him.

"Fine." His voice was rough, like it had been raked over hot coals. "But if I sense you are in danger, I *will* come for you. Nothing will stand in my way."

"I know." She tilted her head to reach his lips. "Thank you."

Chapter 16
Dana

Dana marched into Judge Larson's makeshift courtroom—a smattering of chairs and desks in the community center—with her cousin by her side. Chrissy was a bang-up attorney, and the only attorney she could afford. Chrissy had contacted Judge Larson and the police chief the moment Dana reached out, stating a gross misuse of the laws based on nothing but small-town ignorance. She'd arranged a private meeting with the judge to discuss the charges being brought forward. Something that would keep Dana from having to relive the incident in front of the man who'd tried to kill her. Something that dignified her as a victim and not the one to blame. The judge, thankfully, had agreed with Chrissy and seemed equally as frustrated with how the police staff had acted.

Like everyone in this area, Judge Larson was more than just a judge. He was a well-known and respected man who had acted in many capacities throughout Dana's childhood. Soccer coach, mail man, city official, grocery store clerk. Even when she'd moved to the city, Judge Larson would greet her every time she was back in town and shopped at the Buy Mart. He was kind but also took no shit from anyone.

"I'll be right back," Chrissy whispered and gave her hand a squeeze. When she returned, she had that practiced lawyer face in full force. She obviously had bad news.

Before she even opened her mouth, Dana spotted it. *Him.*

Jackson.

"He's not supposed to be here!" Dana screeched in a hushed whisper.

"I know. I know." Chrissy's voice was somewhere in between her favorite cousin and her acting lawyer. She took Dana's shoulders and squared her up. "You've got this. You're strong. This changes nothing."

Dana took a deep breath, nodded, and tried to adapt her facial expression to mirror her cousin's. Her heart beat rapidly. She hadn't realized until this moment that she wasn't only angry at Jackson, but afraid of him. She'd been avoiding thinking of it too hard. Even while talking to police officers and family about what happened, she'd been able to disassociate from the actual event. It was surprisingly easy to do since she'd actually had a great time during her break from reality.

Now, looking at his smug face, seeing plainly how he thought he'd gotten away with trying to kill her, it was *real*. It was intimidating.

She fought the nervous urge to clean her glasses. Her thumbs pressed into the palm of her hand. Her body tingled with pins and needles. It was just like before debate competitions when she was younger. Her mom had always insisted she give things like that a solid try, while on the inside she harbored a terrible fear of public performances. Her mom only wanted the best for her, of course, which was why she pushed so hard. She wanted her children to live full lives and have *real* job prospects. One of her mom's unspoken disapprovals was toward Dana's choice in career. It was never said out loud, but it was in her mom's silence whenever Dana brought up her passion.

She tried to tell herself this was just like a debate meet, which she'd always lived through. She would live through this one, too. She was done pretending to fit in the meek little box Jackson placed her in. She was done being the *goody-two-shoes* girl who lowered her voice when she was angry. She held her chin high, even though her hands were slick with sweat under the table.

Whatever had changed, the judge didn't seem too happy about it either. He frowned at Jackson as the clerk stated the pertinent information for the record. As the two lawyers spoke, Judge Larson's frown remained while his full attention was given to both speakers.

Dana tried to listen, but most of her energy was going toward keeping her eyes off the man who'd tried to kill her. She watched the judge instead, barely catching it when Jackson's lawyer stated the plea of not guilty.

"My client can't possibly be guilty of this alleged crime. The police officers didn't find a single mark on her body, not a single scratch! This whole thing is a fabrication, a—"

A wave of terrified screams flooded the park outside the community center. Dana didn't have to glance out the window to know what the screaming was about.

Her stomach sank even as her heart rejoiced. She wasn't sure how he was able to sense her, or how the mate bond worked in general. But he'd felt her fear. True to his word, he was swooping in to retrieve her.

While everyone scrambled to get away from the jaws of her lover's two giant, gnashing heads, she rushed to the window and flailed her arms.

"Rathym!"

Chrissy tugged at her arms and clothes, but Dana shook her off. One of Rathym's blazing pairs of eyes spotted her through the glass, then landed on Chrissy's hands on her. The other set found the true source of her fear.

Like a battering ram, Rathym's head crashed through the ceiling, sending debris and people flying. He landed directly on top of Jackson's whimpering form and pinned him to the desk.

"Rathym, stop, please!"

In a fluid motion, Rathym's body burst through the wall and downshifted simultaneously. He grabbed Jackson by the head like a basketball and raised it as though to smash his skull wide open on the desk.

Dana rushed to grab his wrist. He pinned her with furious, confused eyes, his beautiful double irises swirling with hatred and fear. Hatred for those who meant her harm. Hatred for the man who almost kept them from ever meeting. Fear for her life, her *spark* as he called it, to be snuffed out.

Judge Larson sat frozen in his seat, his skin so pale he looked like he might die from shock. She twisted to face him without removing her hand from Rathym's wrist.

"Mr. Larson, this is Rathym. The man who saved me and nursed me back to health after Jackson tried to *kill* me by *throwing me off a cliff*. He means no harm." She met Rathym's burning stare. "Right?"

With a discontented growl, Rathym loosened his grip on Jackson's head but did not release it. "This man must pay with his life."

Minutes passed. Dana began to worry the judge had actually died in his chair, his body still tremoring with the aftershock, but eventually, Mr. Larson cleared his throat. His hands trembled as he raised a scolding finger, his teeth chattering when he spoke. "That is not how the justice system works, young man."

Young man. That was a gross understatement. From what she'd gathered, Rathym was decently old even by dragon standards.

A pathetic whimpering sound drew her attention to the puny head in Rathym's claws, shrunken under his huge claw-tipped hand. Jackson trembled, tears and blood pooling in the divots of his face, a wet stain on his pants from pissing himself.

Although he didn't stop visibly shaking, Judge Larson bravely heard Rathym's corroboration of her injuries and ordered Jackson to be held until sentencing. Since there were no officers remaining in the makeshift courtroom after fleeing the scene, the judge himself led the criminal out of the room on wobbly knees.

The next moment, Dana found herself in Rathym's arms. He scooped her up like a new bride and let his wings fall open.

"Wait!" She struggled to wriggle free. With her feet planted on the ground, she glanced down at his bare lower half for the first time. She clamored over some rubble to reach the two flags hanging in the corner. "I have to say goodbye to my family. Put this on!"

Even tied together, Rathym had to hold them to keep the flags situated over his cocks. Dana snorted and shrugged. She wouldn't make him do this if not for her mom. If her mom wasn't progressive enough to accept her living with a boyfriend, she sure as hell would have trouble with *this*. Maybe she would start to see Dana for

141

who she really was, and not the *good girl* visage she'd crafted. She wasn't a good girl anymore. She'd had sex with a mythical creature. She'd fallen in love with a dragon, for fuck's sake.

The look of pure aghast on her mom's face proved her point. After a fainting spell, she drunkenly thanked him for helping Dana all the same. Samantha agreed to meet at the tourist shop with Dana's things in the morning, lighting up at the prospect of touring Rathym's lair.

Finally, Dana allowed Rathym to supplant her from the rubble-littered ground. His enormous wings sliced through the sky with powerful gusts that shook the tops of the trees. Dana sat perched atop his left head, gripping his neck with her thighs at the spot where it dipped to connect to his jaw. At first she clung to the two largest horns for dear life, but she quickly became accustomed to the flow of wind licking her face and his steady speed.

Giggling like a child, she held her hands to either side and let vaporous wisps of cloud breeze through her fingers. His right head tilted to peer at her askance. With her arms still outstretched, she threw her head back and shouted into the wide-open sky.

"Awhoooooo!"

Rathym dipped his right head and then rose it in a swooping motion. "Raahhhrrroooorr!"

"Keep them closed," Rathym instructed as they slid down the tunnel entrance. His strong arms landed around her waist from behind. His forked tongue grazed her neck in little wet kisses before he retreated, taking her hand to guide her deeper into the cave.

"What's going on?" Dana giggled. Knowing how blind she was, he'd confiscated her glasses but still insisted she kept her eyes closed. It made her sense of smell seem more potent, and she realized how much she'd missed the earthy smell of the cave.

"Patience, my treasure."

"Wow. I know it's bad when *you're* telling *me* to have patience."

"Hmm." He took her shoulders and urged her to sit. "Open."

Rathym grinned down at her as he placed her glasses on the brim of her nose. He swiveled the soft, padded chair.

The walls were lined with bookshelves full of colorful spines. It took her a moment to realize each cubby was carved directly into the cave wall itself. The floors were lined with extravagant rugs. A stunning coffee table was flanked by similarly lush furniture, including a couch and two armchairs that appeared brand-new and ancient all at once. They were adorned with gold flourishes depicting dragons, elves, centaurs, and other creatures. Directly before her was a beautiful rolltop desk, her typewriter and enchanted quill ready for use.

"Oh, Rathym."

Words were inadequate, so she didn't reach for them. She rose and tucked herself into him, clinging as tightly as she could. The soft reptilian skin of his chest was warm. His hearts beat under her ear. A twitch between her legs told her he was getting turned on by her touch. She reached down and slipped a finger into the waistband of the loincloth.

"I think we can say goodbye to the pretenses of *human decency* in our own home, right?"

Smoke poured from his nostrils. His chest rumbled against her cheek. He wasted no time hooking his claw in the collar of her shirt, ripping it down until all her clothes fell away. Their mouths crashed together in a whirlwind of a kiss.

"I have something to show you, too," she purred, set her glasses on the desk, and lowered to her knees.

The length of his top cock was a marvel, its girth too wide for her hand to grip. This close, she understood why he'd been afraid to hurt her the first time. Her hand shrank in comparison, her thumb at *least* an inch from reaching her longest finger, and that was in between the ridges. Curious, she checked the bottom one. It was the smallest of the two, with a sliver of skin still between her fingers.

Her eyes locked on a vein that pulsed from his swollen sack to the tapered tip of his bottom cock. She followed it with her tongue, relishing in the saltiness of his skin, and flicked her tongue over the bead that leaked from his slit. Because his length was so great, she had to lean forward and back in order to cover his shaft with her saliva. As she slipped the tip into her mouth, her jaw straining around it, she peered up at him from below his top cock, which rubbed its ridges on her nose and forehead.

The look on his face was priceless. A crimson, claw-tipped hand covered hers, helping her stroke him just how he liked. Once she had the rhythm down, his hand disappeared into her hair, the other going to his top cock, which he languidly tugged himself against her face, rubbing his cock over the bulge in her cheek.

"What a beautiful sight you are, my treasure." His voice was hoarse with desire and yet steady, as if he were stating facts from the newspaper. "This is a wonderful gift. You're so good to me."

Dana moaned around the mouthful of cock, suctioning her cheeks and bobbing her head harder at his praise.

"You are doing so well, treasure. Let's see if you can take more."

He cupped her cheek and swiped his thumb in circles on the lump there. Something brushed her inner thighs and she rose to allow him access. His tail gently teased at her slick opening, her folds instantly parting. She moaned around him again as he coated his tail with her liquid and spread it all over her seam, from top to bottom.

She rubbed her clit wildly. Through heavy lids, she

145

watched him stroke his cock right in front of her face. Against her face. On her face. He started to rock his hips into her in time to his tugging, meeting her halfway to stuff his other cock to the back of her throat, little breathless groans seeming to force their way out of him.

"I will fill you with my seed, treasure," he said in that steady, stern voice, "and when you beg for more, you shall have it. This time, I will not spill a drop. I will breed your tight cunt until you are round with everything I have to offer."

Even without her glasses, she could see the way he stared down at her like she was the most entrancing thing he'd ever seen. An alluring treasure he couldn't believe belonged to him.

His tail slipped inside her with ease. She would have moaned, but his cock filled her mouth all the way to the entrance of her throat, so no sound came out. She would have paused to enjoy the sensation, but Rathym took ahold of her hair and bobbed her against his cock, fucking her mouth. Then his tail was gone, and she wasn't even able to voice her protest.

His tail slid back, coating her ass with her own dripping fluid. It teased between her cheeks. Her fingers stuttered their circles on her clit when the tip of his tail breached her asshole, her body clenching around the new sensation.

She leaned back until only the tip of his cock rested on her tongue so she could allow her body to adjust. She clung to him as she steadied herself, willing her body to relax.

"You can do it," Rathym encouraged.

"I know." Her voice was a stranger's. "Don't hold back."

With a primal growl, Rathym replaced her glasses and plucked her from the ground. He headed straight for the blankets, his tail still paving its way inside her. When they reached the blankets, he carefully laid her on her side and nestled himself under her bent knees. He caressed her breasts and kissed down her side, flicking his forked tongue over every inch of her skin.

His soft, wandering touches and loving nips and nibbles set her body aflame. Millions of tingly nerves electrified her skin. It was so tender that she nearly forgot the building pressure that was now deep inside her ass until it was taken away. She immediately missed it, a whimper escaping her that Rathym rushed to steal from her lips.

"Don't fret, my love."

He quieted her with a gentle caress of his tail before slipping it around her neck. Firm, but not too tight. He lifted her bent knee and held it across his torso as he guided his top cock to the heat of her need.

Before he pressed inside like she needed, a warm liquid drizzled over them both. He was pouring some kind of slick oil where they were nearly joined.

"My treasure is determined and skillful. But this will allow you to take both of me, without damaging yourself."

147

Both of him. Her eyes widened. She wanted to be absolutely stuffed to the brim with both of his enormous cocks, but would it work? The shimmering semi-translucent liquid was obviously magic, so she chose to trust him and believe her human body would *magically* be able to allow such a wide load inside without ripping her right down the middle.

Setting the pitcher aside, Rathym slowly eased into her cunt until his head popped in deliciously, sending sparks twinkling behind her eyelids. All of her thoughts disappeared as he leaned down, simultaneously pushing farther into her and kissing the side of her open mouth.

"You are so beautiful. You take me so well."

One swift thrust, then another. On the next, he retreated until only the tip was still inside and rubbed his smooth bottom cock against her ass.

"Oh, god, Rathym."

He ran his claws through her hair, whispering sweet encouragements as he entered both of her holes slowly, pausing to let her adjust. Her body stretched around him impossibly. If not for the magic lube, she would never be able to take both of his cocks like this. Even with the oil, it was almost too much. Discomfort seeped around the edges of the pleasure as her poor little human asshole strained to allow him inside with another cock only a thin sliver of skin away.

A claw traced the side of her face, down her jaw, to nudge her chin toward him. His beautiful double irises held both amazement and concern as he paused inside

148

her, not quite fully sheathed.

"Don't stop." Dana caught his wrist and leaned onto her elbow to peek down at the spot her holes cinched around his cocks, pulling him further in. "Fill me. Please."

His tongue flicked out. Swirls of gold and crimson seemed to swim between his irises. He opened her palm and sprouted one lone little fire that helped her synapses focus on something other than what was going on between her legs. With one long, forceful stroke, he finally granted her wish. She cried out as the blackness behind her eyelids burst with streaks of color that continued to blur her vision when she opened them again.

If she'd been grateful for the lube before, she was even more so now. The sting of pain was gone, and all that was left was mind-numbing pleasure, almost too much to bear. She was so stuffed, so full, so absolutely past her capacity and then some. With each stroke, the ribs on his top cock stroked hidden places inside her pussy walls. Her moans came out choppy and high-pitched, but she couldn't stop making noise.

"Look how well you're doing, my treasure," Rathym cooed, his firm voice dripping with syrup now. He didn't move, only watched her adjust patiently, running his finger down her belly where the ridges of his cock were buried. "I knew you could do it."

All she could do was mewl. Slowly, he started to move. Her head lolled against his tail as she tried unsuccessfully to keep her eyes open. She wanted to watch him fuck her ass and her cunt, but each time he plunged into her again, her eyes fluttered closed. He impaled her with his cocks over and over, holding her knee against him with one hand, the other holding her hip stationary.

Rathym was in total control. He delved deep inside of her with both of his cocks, their bodies smacking wetly against each other. She was so *full*. More full than humanly possible.

His tail settled around her waist, the tip of it stroking her clit as he plunged deep into her stomach, all the way up to her guts, possibly *past* them with the magic lube. The sensation sent her over the edge, her panted moans silencing with blinding waves of pleasure. Her body went rigid, but he didn't stop. He fucked her mouth, her ass, her cunt, never missing a stroke even as her orgasm made her go limp.

"I'm going to fill you with my seed. Are you ready, my treasure?"

She couldn't respond. He lifted her hips, the new position allowing him even deeper than before. Her clit throbbed against the smoother plates of his abdomen, which she could feel overlapping and shifting with each of his movements.

She grabbed his horns for support as his cocks reached so high inside of her that, without the oil, she would die from the pounding of her organs if she hadn't ripped in half already.

150

He held her still, like a lifeless doll whose only purpose was to swallow up his come with its body. The thought made her body clench around him, needing to be his little fuck doll, needing to receive every last drop of his seed, just like she was made for. She was made for this, for him, her body a vessel for his pleasure and a receptacle for his come.

The cock inside her pussy gave way first. A tidal wave of his come rushed into her nonstop, but Rathym didn't slow, even as the slap of his corpulent sack became sticky against her ass. His head reared back and he growled so fiercely it was more like a roar. He continued to drive into her relentlessly, using her motionless body to siphon every drop of come into her starving holes.

His arms tensed around her. She could feel his muscles fighting to continue using her pliant body to milk himself. She felt him draining inside of her again, the surge of warm liquid causing her body to fall over another cliff and cascade down the wall of yet another orgasm.

His body weighed down on hers as he continued to rock his hips with his release. As his body sagged, she gripped the bedding and clenched around his cock, rocking her hips and squeezing her inner muscles to force every last drop inside of her. She looked down and gasped at the sight of her belly, so full with his come that it ballooned out around his cock and sloshed with her heavy breaths.

151

"We're going to need a bath every time we do this." She giggled.

Rathym grunted an agreement and kissed along her neck as they caught their breath. A few moments later, he swiftly carried her to the waterfall, not letting her even attempt to walk. Which was definitely necessary.

When they returned, he carried her to the plush swivel chair and pulled one of the armchairs around to watch over her shoulder. They remained that way for the rest of the day until her head drooped over the keys.

Chapter 17
Rathym

"**D**o you think they'll like me?"

"Of course. You are my mate," Rathym stated plainly, though he was nervous as well. Not that his friends wouldn't like her—it didn't matter if they did, but he knew they would anyway—but because he needed to explain his reaction a few weeks ago, on the day of the reckoning. "Besides, you are a joy. If they didn't like you, they would be clods. It's been centuries since I've socialized with them, but I do not believe they've turned into clods."

His words seemed to ease her a little, but she

continued to fuss with the hem of her rose-pink blouse. Every few minutes, she removed her spectacles and ran her cloth over each lens. The next time her hand flew to her face, Rathym plucked it from the air and kissed her knuckles. He kept her hand in his as he used the other to knock on the door.

Moments later, the door swung open and a shocked Anabraxus stood with her hands over her mouth. "Rathym? Why is Rathym on my doorstep?"

Dana sent Rathym a panicked glance. "Did you not tell them we were coming?"

"Oh, he didn't need to. I'm just not used to him accepting my invitations!" Anabraxus threw back her head and laughed. "Come in, come in!"

Once inside, the living quarters opened into a vaulted ceiling tall enough for two dragons to live in comfortably in either shift, with a long hallway peppered with wide doorways. Rathym had always thought he would live like this, in a cozy home with breathing room plus a tad extra. The furnishings were tasteful and homey, their modern style was nothing like Rathym's cave.

"And you must be Rathym's mate," Ana crooned. "We're so glad the cantankerous old lump found someone."

Rathym glowered at his old friend, but she only laughed and winked.

"How about some tea?"

Without waiting for an answer, Ana retreated to the

kitchen and returned with a tray. Just as she set it on a dining table that was clearly too high for humans by the way Dana's arms reached for her teacup, Ryuu's thundering footsteps came from the end of the hall. After a pause, the footfalls lightened, faded back, then returned. Ryuu rounded the couch in a garment and a surprised smile.

"You really showed up. And with your date!" Ryuu beamed at Dana, taking her hand abruptly and kissing the back of it. "Charmed to meet you! We thought the day would never come!"

"This is Dana. Dana, this is Ryuu, and his wife, Anabraxus." He knew his friends meant well, but the *cantankerous* old Rathym wasn't the persona he wished to be known as anymore. Of course, his friends wouldn't know that until they all became reacquainted with one another. "I was hoping for your hospitality while we're in town for the celebration."

His friends exchanged a look. Anabraxus was the first to recover. "Of course. We'd love the company. I'm in need of a shopping companion, if you're interested, Dana?"

Dana lit up, her whole being radiating with excitement. "I can't wait to see the shops!"

"Before you leave," Rathym cleared his throat, "I would like to explain my actions on that day."

He didn't need to say *which* day. The room sobered immediately. Ana dropped her hand from his shoulder and stood beside Ryuu, both of them meeting his gaze

155

with somber expressions.

"Rathym, you don't need to explain," Ryuu said softly. "Luvon was dear to you. Of course the reckoning was inadequate."

Ana nodded. "It was bullshit, honestly."

"I appreciate that, my friends. I would still like to say how grateful I was for your presence. For a long time, I thought vengeance was what I needed. That the death of his murderer would bring me peace." Rathym squeezed the hand Dana had placed on his thigh. "I've come to learn that closure does not come from any external event. I could have had it this whole time. I was stubborn and foolish, but most of all, afraid. I could have been a better friend. Instead, I hid, and for that I am sorry."

It was difficult to meet their eyes, so full of sympathy, but he forced himself to anyway. Ana was the first to lean toward him, and then they both embraced him.

"It's okay. You're here now."

Dana's hand slipped from his and she tossed her arms around him as well. Ana laughed and broke the hug, both her and Ryuu's eyes glistening with unshed tears.

"Right, then. Shall we be off?" Ana asked, though it wasn't a question. She took Dana's hand in hers and marched to the door.

Rathym watched them walk away, Dana's bright smile warm as the Great Flame.

"Wait." He sauntered up to his beautiful mate and

156

pulled her flush against him. It didn't matter that his friends were there, ogling his display of affection. He tilted her chin up and claimed her mouth, slowly, reverently. When he stepped back, she wobbled on her feet and his breath came in little smoky pants.

"I love you."

"And I you, my treasure." He kissed along her jawline and murmured in her ear, "I am yours. We belong together."

Chapter 18
Dana

The extensive stone street was endless, seamlessly weaving through the dunes like oil in water. Colors and textures and delicious smells flooded all of Dana's senses. The entire market square was obviously designed for dragons, with high-reaching walls broad entryways. Most of the buildings either didn't have roofs or had a sheen-like veil of magic that acted as the ceiling.

Although the architecture heavily favored dragon-kind, there were lots of accommodations for other species. Dana had almost tripped on a circular puddle about one inch deep and a foot long that was carved directly into the floor of a bath shop and smelled like sea salt and full clouds. When she asked Ana about it, she'd explained that there was a rising population of sirens and näcken, both of which required salt water dips to survive.

"What's a näcken?"

"Water spirits with a whole culture around music. Some of them can shapeshift, too. There's one who plays the violin at the pavilion every now and then. If they're out today, we'll have to stop and listen! Their voices are angelic."

Most of the shops had small sections carved out for non-dragon customers, but not all of them. It was very clear that this was a city eager to become inclusive. Most of the citizens and shop owners were kind and ready to help Dana cobble together a wardrobe. She'd brought a dress that she'd fully intended to wear, but with Ana's cajoling, she decided to splurge on something unexpected to surprise Rathym with.

"What about this one?" asked Ana, holding up a champagne-and-plum gown fit for royalty. The fabric seemed to scintillate like scales in moonlight.

"That's fucking beautiful! But I don't see anywhere for my arms to go?"

"Ahhh," the shopkeeper cooed. "This garment was created for a particularly picky naga who was more snake than woman. Let me see."

Ana handed the stunning dress to the flaxen dragon, who held it up against Dana's torso. Over her shoulder, Dana saw her reflection in the dragon-sized mirror. She couldn't help but laugh at what she saw. The beautiful woman in the mirror couldn't be her. Whoever the

159

doppelgänger was, they looked gorgeous.

"This garment can easily be tailored. It could be transformed into any neckline you prefer, although I would suggest a narrow V-line for someone of your frame and bust."

Dana glanced at Ana in the mirror, whose wide eyes mirrored her own giddy excitement.

"Could it be ready by the ball?"

"Of course! Come by at daybreak for a final fitting."

"Thank you! How much will I owe you?"

"You are Sir Odrydimere's plus-one, hmm? You may have anything you wish in this market. You need only mention his name." The shopkeeper winked, then gathered the beautiful dress and disappeared into the sea of tulle and sequins.

"Rathym is going to lose his shit when he sees you in that."

Dana's skin prickled at the thought of her dragon being unable to keep his claws off her in such a public setting. Would he make it through the ball without losing control of his downshift? She giggled at the thought of his body rebelling at the mere sight of her. The barrage of mental images had her grinning like a sex-crazed fool.

Ana bumped her shoulder and laughed maniacally.

"You really do love him. You know, I think you're exactly what he needed."

"What do you mean?"

"He spent centuries avoiding his feelings. You? You're so easy to read, your mortal pining and human empathies like a….a breath of fresh air. You haven't collected a centuries' worth of regrets and sorrows. You're just *you*, all the time."

Dana watched her new friend stumble for words. She couldn't tell if Ana was complimenting her or not. Ana must have sensed it because she gave Dana a warm smile and shook her head.

"I see the way you ground him. The way he softens around you. I have never, ever seen him that way, and I've known him since he was a boy of thirty years. Basically grew up with him." She took Dana's hand and slipped it under her elbow. "I'm glad you found him. How *did* you two meet, anyway?"

Dana laughed.

"I fell."

"What?"

"I literally tumbled into his cave. *Literally*. My ex pushed me off a cliff. I should have died! Apparently, Rathym had just rearranged that mountain the night before. If not for some of his excavating, I would've died for sure."

Ana's shock gave way to a boisterous laugh. "That's the power of fated mates for you."

Dana laughed harder, although she still didn't fully understand the mate bond. Once their laughter died down, an ephemeral sound floated through the air. Ana sped up, pulling Dana along.

"That's them! Do you hear that violin? Let's get closer."

The näcken was strewn over an intricate fountain statue, their finned legs and feet engulfed by water. The violin emitted a sorrowful sound, the song mournful and beautiful at the same time. Their entire existence emanated a deep love and deep grief that immediately brought tears to Dana's eyes. All she could think was that this woeful sound must have been how it felt inside Rathym's hearts for centuries.

"So incredibly talented," she murmured as she wiped her eye.

"They really are. Okay, let's go grab Ryuu and Rathym and convince them to buy us food somewhere!"

That evening, after they returned to the house and said good night to Ana and Ryuu, Rathym pulled her close and nuzzled her hair. Dana's eyes fluttered closed, glad to finally be back in his arms with some privacy.

Too quickly, he withdrew. She pouted and started to turn, but the pad of his claws held her shoulders.

"Patience, treasure. I have a gift for you."

A game. Ever since the day he'd flown her home after Jackson's botched hearing, they'd made a game of trading *gifts*. Sometimes those gifts were tangible items. Sometimes they were their bodies, splayed out in provocative ways, ready for the giving—and taking.

Dana wet her lips, her smile giddy and heart-thrumming. Rathym was *very* good at this game.

"It is a two-part gift. For part one, open your hand."

She obeyed, holding her palm up in front of her, eyes closed. The first gift was something made of hefty metal that felt warm against her fingers.

"Open your eyes."

Before looking down, she glanced at Rathym and was surprised to see a twinge of raw vulnerability. When she looked down, it became clear.

"A key."

She turned the key in her hands. It was ornamental in its craftsmanship. The head was welded to look like the flame of a candle. Along the blade were intricate notches nothing like the plain door keys she'd ever seen. It was a work of art. But what did it go to? Her heart flipped.

"Are you sure?" she asked. "We can wait—"

"Ah, ah. There is another part to the gift."

She followed him out the door and down the street. Orbs of magical fire lit their path. They passed a few other couples taking a stroll in the pleasant night air. Even though the temperatures were beginning to slope downward, it was always warm in the kingdom, with floating fire orbs or campfire-style mounds of enchanted flames.

"Where are we going?"

"Not much farther now."

A few moments later, Rathym tugged on her hand

and turned her to face him.

"My dear treasure, my hearts belong to you. Not so long ago, I thought I had a claim on you because you fell into my lair. How very wrong I was." Little licks of fire sparked inside his double irises. A puff of smoke escaped his nostrils. "My cave is no place for a treasure as important as you. But this might be."

He gently nudged her shoulder and allowed her to turn. Tears were already threatening to fall from his words, but when she saw the beautiful home, they rushed from her eyes. Just like the other houses in the kingdom, it was built with brick and concrete with a door carved out of stone.

They'd spoken about leaving the cave, but Dana hadn't wanted to push him. She understood that the cave represented something deeper for him, that it had been his means of safety and survival through the all-consuming grief he'd spent centuries living with.

"I cannot take credit for everything. I must admit Ryuu helped with the finer details. If you wish for somewhere else, there was another house closer to the market—"

Dana interrupted him with a deep, passionate kiss. She swallowed up his insecurities, his fears, and took them into her body just as she would devour any piece of him.

"It's perfect," she said against his lips. "Should we…"

She bit his lip seductively and watched the way his

irises flared. In one swift movement, he gathered her in his arms and stretched his wings, flying a foot over the ground until they were at the sturdy stone door.

There were no furnishings inside, just a wide-open ceiling and a long hallway, the floor plan very similar to Ana and Ryuu's. Not that she had much time to look around through Rathym's smoky kisses and roving claws.

Rathym hitched her legs up and carried her to the back of the house, his mouth only leaving hers to nibble her earlobe with his fangs. She pressed sloppy kisses along the scales of his neck, their texture making her lips tingle.

"I hoped you'd respond this way." Little furls of smoke puffed from his nostrils as he spoke. Every glimpse inside his mouth sparked with cinders. "Just in case I was right, I came prepared."

He turned around, allowing Dana a full view of the enormous urns with the *Xerald's Interspecies Elixir* logo. The sight filled her core with excitement, her hips rolling against Rathym's abdomen of their own accord.

"You know me so well," she mewled.

"Yes. I know how my treasure likes to be stuffed past capacity. I know that she loves when I fuck every one of her little human holes. She loves to be more full than her poor little body was designed to be."

Dana groaned at the sound of his voice saying everything she wanted in this very moment. She fumbled with the hem of her shirt—which was more like a *tunic*

165

due to the style in the kingdom—as Rathym pinned her against the wall. He held her firmly and tore her panties underneath her skirt. His loincloth fell easily, and then she felt the ridges of his top cock against her slick folds.

They groaned in tandem. The ridges of his cock teased her clit, and she quickly became wet enough that he easily slid back and forth between her thighs. Rathym lifted his saturated cock and slipped his next one through her liquid heat. She gripped him and used her fingers around his cock to guide it in little circular motions against her clit. At the familiar caress of his tail along her cheek, she tilted her head against the wall and opened wide.

"Show me how far you can take my tail into your throat, little treasure."

He spoke with a sultry voice, but she knew it was a command. She loved when he used that tone, so saccharine and yet unforgiving. It made her want to do anything he asked, to give her body to him like the strings of a marionette. So she opened wider and softened her throat muscles, allowing him to push farther inside until tears formed in her eyes.

"You're doing so well," he cooed as his tail pushed past the barriers of her throat. "Swallow."

It didn't seem possible. But he was using *that* tone, so she tried, and somehow her throat contracted around him, making her breathe frantically through her nose.

Rathym groaned. His bottom cock was slathered in her juices now and his top one dripped a trail of pre-come on her fingers. He pulled his tail from her mouth with care before sinking his smooth bottom cock into her pussy.

"Your cunt was made for my cocks. Can you feel how it wants to swallow me whole?"

"Y-yes. It's yours."

"What's mine, treasure?"

"My cunt is yours," she gasped as he jammed another inch inside her.

"What else?"

"My mouth. My asshole. My body."

"That's right. You are my treasure. I love to fuck my little treasure, to see how much her body craves my seed, swallows me completely in every tight hole."

Dana moaned. His bottom cock was close to filling her up to her guts while she held on to his horns for dear life. No matter how many times they'd made love, the first few strokes were still a little painful. Rathym was always gentle and slow until her body adjusted. He'd once used the oil before any penetration, but she found she liked to savor his entry the normal way, despite the discomfort. The pain was part of it, a part she didn't want to give up.

He retreated and easily slid her up the wall as he kneeled before her. Her legs crossed around his neck and he dangled his tail just out of reach of her tongue as he covered his face in her slickness, then ran his long tongue from her dripping slit to her taut bud. She whimpered and squirmed against his face, clinging to his horns.

"That's not fair."

Rathym's claws pressed into her thigh as he held her still, ignoring her complaint. He licked her seam again, this time ending with his mouth suctioned against her clit. He sucked rhythmically, his groan vibrating through her like a tuning fork.

When he lowered his tongue to lick her again, he plunged it deep inside and licked her inner walls like it held the last drop of water in a desert.

"Rathym," she cried. "Fuck me. Please."

Just like that, he was standing before her again, his ridged cock replacing his tongue. Dana moaned, and he took advantage of her pleasure by sinking the rest of his cock all the way inside, forcing her body to accommodate his great size.

Once her breathing returned to normal, he slowly rocked his hips back just an inch, then sank into her again. She glanced down at where they were joined, where her pussy clutched his cock desperately. When he rocked his hips back again, she watched the bulge in her belly move lower, then surge back up, visual proof of how deeply he filled her. She placed a hand on her stomach to feel his cock fuck into her through the layers of skin.

Rathym held her against the wall with one arm. His other hand rolled and pinched her nipple. Her breath hitched, her body almost going limp when he replaced his hand with his mouth.

Moments later, she felt his hand against her ass, wet

with the magic oil, which felt more like real fluids than the lubes she'd ever come across before. His tongue moved on to her other nipple, sucking and nibbling, his fangs brushing her sensitive skin.

"Are you ready, my treasure?" he cooed. Although he phrased it as a question, she knew what it really was. A warning.

"Ye-yes. Fill me."

"Is that what you want? You want both of my cocks stuffed into your little holes?"

"Yes. I want your cock in my ass."

Immediately she felt the pressure of his bottom cock against the ring of muscle around her asshole. The lump in her belly retreated to the bottom of her navel as he lined himself up.

"Breathe, treasure."

She took a full breath and let it out slowly, willing her body to relax.

"Another."

She obeyed. On the exhale, he pushed the tip of his bottom cock inside her ass, simultaneously pressing farther into her cunt.

The groan that escaped her lips was not sexy. It was carnal and involuntary, deep and unrecognizable. Rathym matched her with his own primal growl, a bestial sound that sent vibrations through their connection. He dipped down and sucked her nipple, using his tongue to press it against his fang while he held still to allow her to adjust. Even with the magic lube, her body needed to

169

loosen to allow him inside.

When she felt her body was ready, she rocked her hips to signal him. He met her eagerly, shoving both of his cocks farther inside, the thin wall between them all that kept him from ripping her apart.

"I'm so proud of you." His breath was extra hot against her neck. "You take my cocks like the good little treasure you are."

Her orgasm was quickly gaining speed. The sounds she babbled were desperate, frantic. She could feel how full her body was, full to capacity and then some. He leaned in to kiss her and the bulge of his cocks rubbed against their stomachs, adding another delicious sensation. Rathym must have felt it, too, because he let out an animalistic growl.

"You're doing so well. Take my tail into your mouth. You deserve it."

She was beyond the ability to move, her body limp, only his strong arms and the sturdy wall keeping her from collapsing into a puddle on the floor. She opened her mouth and relished the way he fucked to the back of her throat. She loved how well he knew her. He knew she was not capable of anything right now, that she was only a vessel for his many fuckable appendages, and he knew that she absolutely *loved* to be his fuck toy.

The thought of him using her, fucking her holes while she was utterly immobilized, along with the overly stuffed sensation in her core, made her orgasm race through her without warning. For a moment he continued to fuck her throat, and then he retreated to allow her to breathe through the blinding contractions. Her vision went black, intense and overwhelming pleasure the only thing she could feel.

"Very good, treasure. Come around my cocks. Once you are done, you'll be rewarded. Everything you want will be yours." His thumb circled her clit and her body hummed like a buzzing beehive dripping with honey.

When consciousness finally dropped back into her body, he grabbed two handfuls of her ass and maneuvered them to the floor, his back against the wall, her body draped over his. The change in position touched new spots within her, another orgasm thrumming her taut muscles like a ceremonial harp. He slammed her up and down on his cocks repeatedly, milking himself with her limp body, as she gripped his horns like handlebars to remain upright.

"Very good. You have been such a good treasure. Now you will take every drop of my seed. You've earned it."

Every word he spoke made her mewl, a string of incoherent moans pouring from her as freely as the praise seeped from his tongue. She loved to be good for him. The final aspect of her life where she was a *good girl* was here, on his cocks, his deep voice whispering in her ear.

Although she was on top of him, she could do nothing but remain loose so he could bounce her on his cocks. He easily used her body to siphon the come from his swollen sack, through the base of his pulsing shaft, until she felt him erupt inside of her like a molten wave.

He did not slow. He held her body still and fucked up into her until a puddle grew on the floor, splashing between them wetly with his wild motions.

When the cock deep in her asshole gave way, she was already riding the conveyer of another orgasm. As both of his steady streams coursed through her, she lost connection with her body again as it was sent through another round of convulsions. Rathym leaned his head against the wall, pulling her tight against his chest. Still, he did not fully stop moving. He thrust into her with stuttered twitches of his hips while their come smacked against their skin, her body way past full.

Rathym nuzzled her neck, the purr coming from his throat a gentle reminder that was a balm to her very soul. Even when he was lost in the throes of passion, his deep, demanding voice undeniable, she knew his hearts belonged to her.

Chapter 19
Rathym

On the morning of the memorial ball, Rathym awoke to his favorite feeling in all the realms.

His greatest treasure lay curled under his claw, her dainty hand appearing extra small as it clutched a long talon. The warmth her body generated was more than her hot-blooded human anatomy. It was his very life source, the pure energy of the sun, a wildfire greater than any stream of magma the Great Flame produced. It was everything. *She* was everything.

He downshifted and pulled her close. Her body easily molded to his, fitting in his arms like it was made for him. Perhaps at one time he would have thought that the case, he'd been a disillusioned fool then. She was not made for him, nor did she belong to him because of a silly rule a long-dead greedy old dragon had scribed in an official document.

She was his because she *chose* him, even after all he'd done to push her away. She had stayed, not because he forced her to, but because she saw right through him, saw his fear for what it was. He hadn't lived a single day for two centuries until she came along to wake him from his daze. He'd been a shell waiting for the spark of a mortal who would teach him how to be whole again.

He was made for her. He belonged to her, mind, body, and spark.

Dana roused slowly. He kissed the drowsiness of sleep from her eyes until they opened, her luscious mouth curving at the corners. He shivered as she touched his cheek with feather-soft fingers, trailing them up his temples to skim the top of his spiked crown.

"Good morning, my treasure."

"Good morning. What were you just thinking about?" She giggled as he kissed her nose. "You had your thinking face on."

"I have a thinking face?"

"Yes. And a concentration face. And a brooding face."

"I don't brood."

She snorted and rolled her eyes. "Just answer the question."

"I was thinking about how wrong I was for ever staking claim to you. I'm lucky you stayed around."

"You weren't wrong. Well, you were, but it became true." She slid her hand into his and kissed along his knuckles. "You just didn't know *you* belonged to *me* too."

While dragon-kind had more fluid ideas of decency, it seemed the kingdom had adapted to accommodate the sensibilities of the different species now living among them. The ball would be a mixed bag of party guests and therefore required a certain level of care.

Besides, Rathym was used to wearing a drape of fabric over his lower half by now. Although he and Dana spent most of their time nude while at home, he'd attended her to the human law office a couple of times, and even a family game night, which had been fun after her mother finally quit fainting.

The loincloth he wore now was more extravagant than he cared for, but Ana had sneaked it to him when the two women returned from their morning trip to the shops. While Dana was busy getting dressed, Ana had hissed that he *had* to wear this one to complement Dana's new ball gown. He'd relented and even allowed his friend to adorn his crown with glittery jewelry while he grumbled.

"Just wait until you see her dress. Then you'll get it. You would've looked like a schmooze next to her," Ana whispered with a laugh.

When the door to the guest room squeaked open, Rathym's breath lodged in his throat.

Anabraxus was right. Dana was a goddess. The pattern of the dress shimmered like a frozen lake in the sunlight, their transient colors bleeding and swirling with every rustle of the garment. It hugged her trim body in the most alluring way, a slit of fabric revealing one leg from mid-thigh to ankle. The gentle gold undertones and purple orchid-colored embroidery enhanced her radiant skin, which looked even more enticing with the blush gracing her cheeks.

"Do you like it?" Dana asked timidly.

Rathym clamped his hanging jaw shut and reached for her. He was speechless. He nodded and shook his head helplessly.

"I cannot—I now understand why Ana felt the need to spruce me up."

Dana laughed with him and met his lips for a tender kiss. He cradled her head gently, not wishing to disrupt any face paint she might have on, but she threw herself into his arms.

The New Illuminated Ballroom was at the farthest edge of the kingdom, on the land bordering the decayed remains of Elvendale. Rathym understood why the elves had chosen this location, but it was still difficult. It would remind everyone of the great loss, and the exceptional failure of the Great Flame Kingdom to protect and assist their allies. For Rathym, it was painful for those reasons and more.

"Are you all right?" Dana inquired from her spot on his left head. He hadn't realized he'd started hovering in the air above the ballroom building. From here, he could see the spire of the old Illuminated Ballroom, all the way in the center of the barren, charred land, its walls crumbled and foundation destroyed by the rot.

"It's difficult to bear," he admitted as he downshifted, swiftly maneuvering her to his arms as he touched ground. "I haven't had the courage to come here since…"

Dana kissed his chest, then laid her cheek against his palpitating hearts. She stayed there silently, her touch soothing and understanding, until he was finally able to rip his eyes away.

"Shall we join the party, my treasure?"

The ballroom was enormous, much larger than the old one, and yet Rathym was sure it would feel empty without Luvon's vivid spark if not for Dana's presence beside him. Couples danced and swayed to the grand sound of the orchestra, which filled the room from polished floor to painted ceiling. The beauty of the ballroom was only rivaled by the stunned look on Dana's face, her reaction to the lavish theater more enchanting than anything in all the realms.

Rathym was out of practice with dancing, but his feet found the rhythm quickly. He twirled and spun with his treasure on his arm, following his lead. The twinkle in her eye blazed straight into his inner flame. It was as though her brown eyes were a window to her spark, her life-force brightening the very colors of the room.

During a particularly intimate song that coaxed dance partners closer to one another, Dana pressed her warmth against him, her body encased in his. The feeling of her so close made his cocks twitch, eager for attention, which they could typically expect when his mate was this close. Rathym tried to ignore them, but Dana nuzzled his chest, which only made things worse. Not to mention the scent of her desire, which wafted up to his nostrils and sent his thoughts spiraling through images very inappropriate for the very public setting.

"Careful, treasure, or I will take you right here on this dance floor."

"Do it."

Her answer was unhelpful. His cocks taunted him, too, telling him to heed her words.

With a growl, he scooped her up and marched out of the ballroom, through the entryway, and out the door, only stopping once he reached the back of a neighboring building. From here, they could still hear the party guests who milled about outside, some just now arriving. If he leaned back, he could even see them, just like a curious guest would be able to spot them if they tried.

Rathym pinned her against the brick building and

brought his tail to her mouth.

"Suck on this and be silent. You leave me no choice but to fuck you right here, so be a good treasure and take my cocks quietly."

Before the moan he saw building in her could surface, he slipped his tail into her open mouth and dropped to his knees. He lifted her thighs until they straddled his face, carefully pulling aside the long slit in her dress to reveal the treasure hidden beneath. Her precious cunt was already glistening. He lapped at the sweet liquid, then flattened his tongue against her folds until they split apart.

Dana's hands flew to his horns. She used them as leverage to drive her cunt over his face, and he closed his eyes. For a moment, he relished the way she tried to wrest control of her orgasm, rubbing her swollen clit over his tongue, but he quickly took hold of her thighs to force her still. When she tried to moan in protest, he pushed his tail farther into her mouth.

"This is your fault. You will be patient."

He suctioned his mouth against her clit and slid two fingers inside. This time, his treasure was good and did not make a sound, only tightened her grip on his horns. He sucked and swirled his tongue against her bud as he slipped another finger inside.

He could feel her struggling to stay still. He allowed her a little movement, loosening his hold so she could fuck herself on his fingers and mouth, but he pulled away before she came undone. He watched ravenously as her slick and his saliva dripped down the seam of her ass, both of her tight entries fluttering, searching for him.

"You're doing so well. Now you will take my cocks. Remember, you must be quiet."

He positioned himself between her legs. Nearby, he heard laughter and music pouring from the ballroom, but he didn't bother to glance away. Even if they were spotted, he wouldn't stop.

He gingerly hiked her skirt above her waist, careful not to rip it. He held it up in one hand, the other holding her steady against the wall. He replaced his tail with his tongue, exploring the inside of her mouth as he lined up with her slickness.

He pushed inside slowly, swallowing every cry from her lips. She was tight, so tight, not as prepared as he liked her to be. He didn't want to hurt her. He tried to go slow, to ease inside her delicate human cunt, but she used her legs to drive him inside.

Their groans were not discreet. Rathym pulled away to chastise her, but she rolled her hips, making him lose the words, so he pounded into her instead.

This time, her moan escaped.

"Be quiet, treasure." He punctuated his point with another brutal thrust. "Someone might hear."

"Let them watch."

That little sentence drove him closer to release. He tugged the top of her dress down and drew her nipple into his mouth, nipping the flesh around it with his sharp teeth. She reacted exactly as he'd hoped, her hands tight against his horns, her hips rolling desperately. When he moved to her other nipple, she went rigid, silent.

"That's it, little treasure. Come on my cock. This is what you wanted."

He felt her body obey his command, her inner walls clenching and squeezing, coaxing him to do the same. His release rushed forth, so swift that it stilled his movements and all he could do was press her against the wall and heave as he emptied his cock inside her greedy cunt.

His bottom cock leaked onto the ground, drips of white painting the grass below Dana's ass. Some primal part of him bristled at the waste. As soon as the torrential stream inside her slowed to a dribble, he pulled it out and slammed the second one inside, some of his creamy seed gushing out of her before he plugged her back up.

"Oh my god—" she mewled.

"Quiet!"

It only took one thrust before he was filling her with more of his eager come. He rutted into her like a crazed fool, shoving his cock as far up as it would go, planting his seed deep into her womb.

When they both stopped writhing, he sucked on her earlobe, then trailed little kisses all the way to her mouth.

Dana giggled against his temple.

"You don't expect me to return to the ball with all this dripping down my legs, do you?"

"I didn't have time to consider that."

She laughed harder now. "I figured not."

That night, they slept in their empty new home. Even though they'd made love once or twice more before going to sleep, Rathym woke to his insatiable treasure in the middle of the night, arms and legs strewn over his full-size dragon cock. His cock lengthened until it was easily as long as she was tall.

His hearts fluttered at the appetizing sight. Humor lit within his ribcage to mingle with the adoration that always resided there. There was nothing his treasure could do that he would not find endearing. This was the thought that went through his head as he felt the slick trail from her cunt growing, coating a small spot of his shaft with her sweet nectar.

Once she finished humping him, he used his left head to nudge her back under his claw. This little occurrence happened at least once a week with his ravenous treasure.

He hoped it never stopped.

Epilogue
Dana

Exhausted from the book signing, Dana flung herself onto Rathym's left neck and pulled herself up by his horns.

"I'm so tired. Maybe I should text Addy and reschedule."

"You've been quite animated about this meeting for some time. Don't cancel on your friend. Sleep on our way there."

She sighed. He was right.

Last week, she'd had a video chat with her cover artist and her husband, a demon, to celebrate her success and go over the designs for her brand-new trilogy. The Wi-Fi in the Kingdom of the Great Flame was spotty, but as long as she didn't have other tabs open it worked fine. It was a fair trade for a home with proper plumbing.

Her first cozy mystery series starring a loose representation of Rathym and herself had blown up much quicker than she'd expected. *Scales and Handcuffs* was a hit with the creatures in the kingdom, too. She felt so blessed to have stumbled upon an amazing cover designer whose relationship looked a lot like theirs.

This evening, they would meet Addison and Traeyr in person for the first time. They lived all the way down in Florida, so she had plenty of time for a nap. She fell asleep on Rathym's broad head and only woke when he downshifted, maneuvering her weight into his arms.

"I believe we're here."

Her feet sank into the sand and she squinted in the darkness. The oceanfront home had lights strung along the porch, where a mattress leaned against the wall and a table was set for four. A furry, horned beast and an auburn-haired woman swayed from side to side, dancing to music Dana couldn't hear.

"That's definitely them." She smiled broadly. She had a feeling they were about to take another step toward a lifelong friendship.

Traeyr glanced up at their appearance and nudged Addy. He remained on the porch while Addy slipped out of her flip-flops to run and greet them.

"You made it!" She laughed and guided them to the porch. She motioned to the two men and said cheerily, "You guys wore the same thing. Party foul?"

Dana glanced between their loincloths and laughed along with Addison, but the guys both narrowed their eyes.

"This is elven leather," Rathym informed them, looking affronted.

"I was unaware anything was left from the elves." Traeyr sounded rather impressed. "Very nice."

Dana and Addy stifled more laughter at the innocent exchange.

The night passed with lots of shared laughter and some masculine displays of magic. Rathym had brought his enchanted wine bottle, and before they were all too deep into their cups, the women got to enjoy a performance of shadow and fire. Rathym skillfully danced in the sand with his flames while Traeyr stood at the edge of the porch, sending tendrils of shadow to tell stories of his travels. Somehow, the two men, both well-traveled, shared many favorite destinations.

"Sometimes I still feel guilty for being the reason he can't travel," Addy whispered to her over the shadow-licked table.

"He loves you. He chose this, right?" Dana put her hand over Addy's. "But I get it. Rathym had to change his lifestyle pretty drastically for me, too. You know we've been living in the Great Flame kingdom for a while, and he just organized his hoard so I stopped tripping on random chunks of gold *last week*?"

Addy snorted. Their hushed giggles drew attention, and the men dropped their magic to join them at the table.

"It's getting late. Are you all right to fly, Rathym?" Addy asked.

"I would not endanger my beloved by getting too drunk to fly," he scoffed, then hesitated a moment before looking at Traeyr. "You know, my friend, there are surviving elves in the kingdom. Should you ever find yourself curious, there is always a room for both of you in our home."

Dana's heart melted at her mate's kind words. He was no longer a grouchy old dragon. His *spark* was bright and burning, so visible to her now that she couldn't believe she'd ever thought of him as a rancorous old man. It was a beautiful sight to behold, watching him heal and grow, witnessing the man—dragon—he'd become once he freed himself of guilt.

Dana woke in the middle of the night. Rathym's enormous, full-size claw rested over her body. Memories of the sex they'd had before falling asleep rose to the surface, awakening the same hunger she always felt around him. She shimmied out from under his claw and crawled lower in the bed to where his bestial appendage lay dormant.

She peppered the tip with kisses, which was easily

bigger than her head, and wrapped her arms and legs around it. A bleary-eyed head lifted from the mattress to peer at her, humor and adoration alight in its eyes.

She rubbed her bare breasts against him, her nipples hard and taut against his slightly coarse skin. It was much bigger and more firm than the old body pillow she used to do this with, and worked much better. Straddling him completely, she moaned and rubbed her slick flesh against him, arching and curving her back to create the friction she craved. She humped his huge dragon cock with wild abandon until she came, leaving a little wet trail on the base of his monstrous shaft.

A long, wide, forked tongue licked the side of her face. He nudged her closer with his snout, guiding her back under his paw, where she fell into a peaceful sleep surrounded by the dragon who'd captured her, and her heart.

The End
Thank you for reading my dirty little romance!
If you like confident, curvy women, plus vampires and crows, you'll love Cassandra and Qadaire's story.
Flip the page for a sneak preview!

If you haven't read book one, Married to the Mahr, you can find it on my website or Amazon. It's a sweet and spicy romance about a sleep paralysis demon and his darling dreamer.

You can find all of my links on the following QR code.

Chapter 1

Cassandra

"**D**on't worry, Zero. I'll be back soon. Maybe today's the day, huh, buddy?" Cass cooed to her Australian Shepherd, her best friend and her only real family. Zero meekly raised his head, floppy tongue lolling out for a goodbye lick. "I love you too, goofball."

Her red hatchback sputtered as it kicked into gear. She sped to the lab and parked haphazardly. She was always in a hurry to get to work. Not because she loved her job, but because the work she was doing was important. Important enough that their typically thin budget had stretched infinitely. Too many families were being forced to say their final goodbyes because of Canine X-3, a vicious disease borne from ticks and

189

passed by nearly any means imaginable, including human carriers. Cassandra was working to end to the pandemic.

The weight of responsibility was heavier than ever. Lately it felt like she was both numb and on fire at all times. Her team was the only pathologist crew in Nebraska working exclusively on Canine X-3 around the clock. They collaborated with teams in other states, as well as epidemiologists and various specialists from other fields, but if treatment was discovered outside of her lab, it might be too late.

Zero's time was running thin. Canine X-3 was a long, slow disease, with more lethargy than pain, which left space for hope.

With her station set up, she crossed the room to pull out her tray of samples. At first glance, they appeared as though nothing had changed, but that didn't phase her. Patience was easy while she was so numb, plus she was confident in her capabilities. She'd fought tooth and nail to get here, and she had the scars and stretch marks to prove it. The extra years of school and the fallout with her family had broken her. She'd shed her identity and redefined herself again and again to get this far. Once when her parents ghosted her. Once when her depression returned in full swing. Once when she and her ex decided to go back to being friends. Once when she decided to go back to school for pathology, only to get so depressed a few years in that she could do nothing but binge and cry, ultimately pushing graduation out an extra year.

She'd lived through all those challenges. More than that, she now proudly thrived as second to the head of her department *because* of those experiences. She would survive this one, too. And by fucking god, Zero would be right by her side.

A crisp breeze sent leaves scuttling outside the window. The tip of her nose tingled. Shouldn't the vents be blowing warm air? She glanced toward them and noticed the wide open window.

If she hadn't caught that oversight, it could have disrupted her work. She slipped off her gloves. The moment she reached for the window, she was assaulted by a flurry of dark, squawking wings. The wild animal rapidly changed course, retreating back through the window and soaring into a tree. She latched the window with a frustrated huff, donned a new pair of gloves, and rounded her workstation again.

A red envelope sealed with blood-red wax lay on her stool. Cass glanced around the room. Empty. She checked the hall. No one.

"What the fuck is going on this morning?"

She slipped her finger through the wax and released the postcard-sized note inside.

I have the answers you seek.
All I request in return is anonymity.
Agree to assume responsibility, and the formula
is yours.

Seriously, what the hell?

Regardless of how shady the letter was, it was tempting. Naturally, she had lots of questions. Why would someone claim to have the formula, but not want to come forward? What would they gain? Was it some kind of scam? They could've at least sent an email. Creepy.

Best to ignore the weird offer and get to work. This peculiar day was already slipping by too quickly. Besides, she wouldn't add plagiarism to her repertoire. That wasn't how she'd gotten this far.

She worked alone for hours until her colleagues began to show up. No words were exchanged past pleasantries delivered with grave faces. By the end of the day, her shoulders were so hunched it cracked her back to stand straight, her soul bruised after another wasted day.

Autumn's tapestry of reds and yellows blurred outside her window through unshed tears. *Splat.* A black-and-white pellet of bird shit smacked her windshield.

"Oh, come on!"

She leaned close to the wheel for a better look. Those damn crows had shown up a couple weeks ago, hanging out around her house and the lab. Didn't crows spend the cold seasons in one place? It was barely the middle of September, so she had a long winter of fat bird poops ahead. Add it to the growing list of crappy things that were out of her control. Pun intended.

There was no *thump, thump* of Zero's tail that greeted

her. He was beneath the coffee table, sleeping like a cat.

"Hey, buddy. Let me change, then I'll read to you, okay?"

After some thorough scratchies, she led him to the bedroom and put on her comfy night T-shirt. With long days in the lab, she pretty much slept, worked, read a bedtime story, and repeat. In all honesty, that wasn't much different than before Canine-X3. Work was dependable, steady, something she could count on. She was damn good at her job and she knew it, even if it was getting harder to remember that lately.

She'd been reading to Zero every night since liberating him from the shelter. Tonight, she was on the last book in her current favorite series, *Scales and Handcuffs*, about a dragon and a human woman finding love and fighting crime. She'd picked it up for the stunning cover, but the story was so beautiful that the author had quickly become a one-click buy. The amount of love between the main characters was so electric, Cass could almost pretend she was a part of it.

The filthy yet poetic words of a love scene made her giggle as she read them aloud. Zero's soft breathing steadily evened as he fell asleep. Cass drifted off soon after, her book slumping over her chest.

In the morning, she woke to eager licks from her chin to her forehead. Months ago, she might've found this wake-up call mildly irritating. Today, she was glad for proof that Zero still had spirit.

At the lab that day, Cass checked the window before

pulling out her supplies. Shut. She locked it, just in case. A crow flew to the ledge, cocked its head to and fro, and leered at her with its beady black marbles.

"You're awfully plucky, huh? Leave it shut this time, little trickster."

She gave it a wink and got to work. As she set up her workstation, the little red letter peeked from under a stack of papers. She opened it, read the words again, and pursed her lips. *On the off chance . . .*

She shook away the ridiculous thought and discarded the envelope into her desk drawer. No. There was no mysterious benefactor coming to swoop in and save the day. There was just her.

She only hoped she was enough.

Chapter 2
Qadaire

"It's your move, my friend."

Qadaire's opponent twitched his head once to the left, once to the right.

"You pass? Again? You'll have to make a move eventually. Perhaps there's something to this game that you understand and I don't."

"Craww." *I forfeit.*

"Ah, yes. There's always that." Qadaire rose from the rectangular mahogany table with a sigh. He ruffled his feathers, stretching his wings outward. With his lower set of hands, he stacked the chips neatly. He pressed his upper palms together and bowed humbly. "I accept your forfeit. I'm sure you'll best me next time."

The crow bristled, then kicked his legs out and hopped to the back of the elaborate red dining chair. Everything in this damned mansion was red. Blood red, extra bloody red, crusty brownish dried blood, all with accents of black, like the blood of the vampires who'd once been occupants. Qadaire had never gotten around to remodeling after killing the tyrant. It wasn't like he would entertain company ever again. Vampiric society had probably forgotten his existence by now or assumed he'd died in the act of killing Dracula VI.

Qadaire was alive and well, and deformed. Not fully crow and not fully vampire. Certainly not human, not even passably. He had one too many pairs of arms, skin the color of ash, and layers upon layers of obsidian black feathers that covered most of his body. His wings matched those of his opponent's, along with all the other crows roosting until spring.

"Let's check on our little project, hmm?"

At least the curse had completed enough to let him converse with the crows. With around two dozen calls, some were translatable and some were not, but he inherently understood them all, even their wordless thoughts. He caught glimpses into their minds. He could also connect to their senses, including their vision, and send small amounts of magic through their connection. This made hunting easy. He didn't prey on humans anymore. He foraged and fed his friends, and in turn, they lent him their sight to locate deer, coyotes, and bears. Without them, he'd likely never have had the rare delicacy of bull moose.

While he'd never bothered to refurnish his home— or cage, he wasn't sure which term was more accurate— he'd been collecting tools and contraptions for the last few centuries. Had it been two or three centuries? Perhaps it was closer to four or five. He'd managed to forget the passing of time by throwing himself into the addictive throes of knowledge. Knowledge was the only thing that lasted. With lifespans of barely over a decade, his crow companions came and went in the blink of an eye. *Knowledge* never left. It could be compounded, multiplied. Shared. Gifted.

"Has she considered my offer?" Qadaire muttered, more to himself than the crow on his shoulder or those in the high rafters of his largest lab.

No, master.

"Still in her drawer? Curious."

By *curious* he meant *implausible.* No one had ever denied his offer. He'd been the benefactor to hundreds of human inventors, biologists, astronomers, archaeologists. Every single one had greedily accepted his terms. He'd singlehandedly stopped multiple pandemics, eradicated polio, and pioneered some of the most acclaimed studies in fields from electrical to environmental. He'd discovered the structure of the DNA strand in this very lab. Some of those sciences were in his past, however, as his glamor skills had waned from lack of use and were now too weak to charm more than one or two humans at a time. Thus, there were certain practices he couldn't participate in anymore, which annoyed him to no end.

Through the view of a crow casually observing the woman in her laboratory, Qadaire watched the gifted pathologist, as he'd been doing for weeks now. She was an intriguing specimen. Aside from her convincing credentials, she was nothing like she appeared on paper. Any passionate intellectual could reach the top of their field, but she was more . . . *tangible.* Her odd characteristics had lit a spark within him. The furrow in her brow as she glared through the microscope. The sideways purse of her lips when she got stuck. The way she patted her thighs—those full, jiggly thighs—when she was stuck longer than she liked. Her painted skin and luscious curves fanned that spark, crackling through him.

Every morning, she breathlessly rushed into her lab as though she'd sprinted all the way there. Sometimes there was a pink twinge to her cheeks and dark puffiness under her eyes, which made their chocolate daylily color more vibrant. Those days, she pursed her lips and swatted her thighs and made little huffy noises more often. Qadaire hypothesized that she had personal reasons for her scholarly rigor. She was too close to the case. Another reason why he was certain she would accept his offer.

He watched the woman—*Dr. Cassandra Billing DVM*—set up her station. She had that *rushed* quality this morning.

"Have we scouted her place of residence?"

While he wouldn't disrespect her privacy by leering himself, he did require a modicum of personal knowledge about anyone he collaborated with. The crows confirmed they had, and indeed, she had a sick pup. Qadaire's chest clenched even as a sly grin tugged his lips.

"You'll see." Qadaire released the string tying his sight to the crow's and clasped his lower pair of hands behind his back. He gestured out of the room with a smile. "Let's have a rematch. She'll be penning a response before we declare the winner."

Made in the USA
Columbia, SC
31 January 2025

52355483R00111